Utopia

D0475870

EVERYMAN,
I WILL GO WITH THEE,
AND BE THY GUIDE,
IN THY MOST NEED
TO GO BY THY SIDE

THOMAS MORE

Utopia

Translated from the Latin
by Ralph Robinson
with an Introduction by
Jenny Mezciems

E V E R Y M A N ' S   L I B R A R Y

61

This book is one of 250 volumes in Everyman's Library
which have been distributed to 4500 state schools
throughout the United Kingdom.
The project has been supported by a grant of £4 million
from the Millennium Commission.

First included in Everyman's Library, 1910
Introduction, Bibliography and Chronology © David Campbell
Publishers Ltd., 1992
Typography by Peter B. Willberg

ISBN 1-85715-061-9

A CIP catalogue record for this book is available from the
British Library

Published by David Campbell Publishers Ltd.,
Gloucester Mansions, 140A Shaftesbury Avenue,
London WC2H 8HD

Distributed by Random House (UK) Ltd.,
20 Vauxhall Bridge Road, London SW1V 2SA

CONTENTS

INTRODUCTION

The most authoritative introduction to *Utopia* is the one which appeared on the title-page of the first edition in 1516, for what else is a title but an introduction? In the case of More's most famous book the title, for all its seemingly purposeful expansiveness, introduces a series of dualisms or oppositions which the reader may at first accept without suspicion; only after the experience of reading will apparent clarities of statement turn into delightful puzzles or vexatious anxieties of interpretation. For the modern reader there is the additional complication that we are usually reading an English transla- tion of a work first written for an English and European audience in the *lingua franca* of Renaissance Latin. The present text, with spelling modernized, has the virtue of being that of the first English translation, by More's countryman Ralph Robinson, in 1551. The vocabulary will seem archaic, requiring some effort from the reader, but the English is that of More's own time (within twenty years) and of a period significant in the development of the vernacular and the history of the language. If we feel that the choice between Robinson's English and More's Latin is a choice between two foreign languages, then the dilemma will be only the first of many, and either way can be enjoyed as a means of approaching Thomas More more closely than we might in ever-changing 'modern' English.

That inviting title of the first edition runs as follows: *Libellus vere aureus nec minus salutaris quam festivus de optimo reipublicae statu, deque nova Insula Utopia*, which can be translated as 'A truly golden handbook, no less profitable than entertaining, concerning the best state of a commonwealth and the new island of Utopia' (the word 'commonwealth' avoids inappro- priate modern senses of the word 'republic', though readers familiar with Plato's *Republic*, an obvious and acknowledged source for the idea of More's book, will be used to thinking in such terms as 'the common weal', or 'the public good'). But the phrases used offer us pairs of concepts, right at the outset.

For the work to claim to be instructive as well as diverting is simply to point to requirements prescribed in the ancient world, memorably and influentially, by Horace and Lucretius; at the same time the phrase allows a suggestion of doubt as to how seriously we should take what we read, and by the end of the book most readers are concerned with just that problem, wondering what More meant us to think of it all: perhaps remembering anecdotes about how those who knew him often didn't know whether he was joking or in earnest; possibly aware of the pleasure with which More and his humanist friend Erasmus of Rotterdam had collaborated on translations of the Syrian Greek-writer Lucian (AD *c.* 117–80), with whose satiric fantasies the concept of *serio ludere* is commonly associated.

Perhaps, after closer acquaintance with More's ambiguities, or deliberate self-contradictions, one should also wonder if there is something oxymoronic about the term 'truly golden', since gold is so regularly associated with deception and false-ness in this text and others of similar spirit. But it may be safer to move on to register the way that 'the best state of a commonwealth' invites one, surely, to think in abstractions – while the first section of the book largely consists instead of sustained criticism of the state of contemporary England, and the second part, dealing with 'the new island of Utopia', is after all fiction rather than fact. A further pairing, or rather one should say opposition, comes for the reader with the discovery that there are two 'authors' or speakers involved in the debate which frames the account of Utopia, and the most notoriously vexing aspect of the work is in the uncertainty as to how far, if at all, one may take Thomas More as being in sympathy with the strong views expressed by his fictional traveller Raphael Hythlodaeus. There is a 'More' who takes part in the fictional discussion – but, readers have argued, it is as clear as More ever allows anything to be that this figure is itself a fiction, not necessarily to be identified with the Thomas More of real life.

Much of the interest of More's book, for the first-time reader at least, is inevitably with the features of his fictional Utopia itself. It may be a sobering experience for the comparatively affluent modern reader, among whom one has to include the average American, European, or even British student, to discover that the less acceptable features of the desirable Utopian life are mainly those that would deprive us of material luxuries or of means to express our individuality. It is clear enough that various forms of individual sacrifice, by modern Western standards, are logically desirable for the good of the society as a whole – for the 'common weal' – but it is hard to submit, even in imagination, to the necessary totalitarian concept which begins in Plato's *Republic* (never to be realized) and has recently been rejected in communist states in the real world; part of the continuing attraction of *Utopia* is that history seems to revolve around it, showing us ever new facets of 'relevance', of sympathy or understanding. Plato, as well as any thinker since, knew what it takes to convince mankind that the good of one and the good of all are identical, and made due allowance for human weaknesses, just as More does. In the (hypothetical) just state, the totalitarian paradise, it is a truism that the interests of state and individual are the same, as though it requires a fiction to resolve apparent conflict into harmony or forge such unity from division. One of the lessons More teaches his reader is the distinction between fiction and fact, hypothesis and contingency, and at a period when the power of the word was so hugely increased by the authority and spread of printed matter, the training of readers in evaluating the truth of what they read is a matter of fairly advanced educational technique. Dominic Baker-Smith in a recent scholarly critical account of More's book reminds us of the way in which the dilemmas of interpretation, which throw such an onus of judgement on the reader, make of the work a characteristically open-ended humanistic exercise, educative not least in its refusal to give us an authoritative 'authorial' voice telling us what to think. But then, the lives of Erasmus and other humanist thinkers were devoted to the undoing of unthinking acceptance of authority: that of the unsatisfactory Vulgate Latin Bible, which made Erasmus go back to the Greek and retranslate; the medial scholastic habit of scoring debating points about trivialities by reference to 'authorities'; the corruption, by exploitation of the gullible masses, of the unreformed Roman Catholic Church, so that the Christian religion could seem a debased dependence of greed and power on superstition rather than any kind of reasoned or reasonable faith.

It is a feature of the Renaissance humanist reforming spirit that the study of Greek (newly fashionable, with More's friend William Grocyn introducing it into the Oxford curriculum) should be used to offer a kind of release from Latin authority, even though Latin necessarily remained the language of universal communication. One of the delights of Greek in this context, surely, is its capacity for ambiguity and its conceptual richness. It is hardly surprising, perhaps, that More and his fellow-humanists, reassessing the world of learning around them, and the foundations of belief, should relish the delights of uncertainty, of the need to replenish and rearrange their intellectual furniture. Hence, most importantly for the text and implications of *Utopia*, the ambiguity of the very name given to the island. It is the first of many puns, and may have been coined by Erasmus, who saw the book through the press in Louvain while More was at home in England. The pun is in the spirit of Erasmus's own slightly earlier work, *The Praise of Folly*, written partly while he was with More in England in 1509, whose title, in either Greek or Latin, makes use of the fact that the Greek word for 'folly' is more or less the same as More's name, so that Folly's praise (of herself) is also the praise of More, the *Moriae Encomium*. There were of course readers incapable of appreciating the ironies and ambiguities of such literary games; a solemn theologian called Martin Dorp, rather like the literal-minded reader More castigates in his own prefatory letter in the *Utopia*, was offended at Erasmus's mockeries, which he mostly misunderstood, in their relation to Christian practices and Christian 'follies', and himself appears a fool when one reads the letters of patient explanation written to him by both Erasmus and More.

The meaning of the word 'utopia' essentially depends on an ambiguity in the translation of Greek ideas into Latin form. For the Greek offers two concepts where the Latin has only the one: 'unplace' or 'no-place'. The Latin fuses together two Greek prefixes, εὖ (good, or even happy) and οὐ (not): so 'eutopia' would mean 'good place'; 'outopia' would mean 'no place'. Latin, as the universal language of the educated world, was the language available for the spread of ideas, but those who learned Greek formed an élite; theirs were the pleasures of such puns and games with language as More and Erasmus, with other like-minded contemporaries, exploit here, perhaps with something like a schoolboyish delight in the novelty of it all. Once rendered into Latin, and impossible to translate into English other than by its tidy single meaning, the original concept suffers by reduction: the word utopia develops into a term which loosely suggests the unreal, the impractical, pipe dreams and pie-in-the-sky, but in a pejorative sense (the good place ought *not* to be unreal), losing the subtlety that made the two concepts definitively interdependent; the essence of a utopia is that it cannot be realized. Before they had the better idea, More and Erasmus had written to each other about their 'nusquama' (nowhere) project – another name for which might have been 'udepotia', from the Greek οὐδέποτε (never). Later writers of dystopias, the opposites of utopias (on the assumption that utopia means eutopia), recognize their pedigree, and the conceptual tradition to which their works belong, by making their imagined worlds not nowhere and never, but in the immediately threatening future (*Nineteen Eighty-Four*) or the spatially familiar local landscape (*Brave New World*). In the same way, when William Morris wanted his Romantic utopia to seem accessible, his *Nowhere* could seem, by allusion to these traditional literary puns of the genre, to offer something 'Now here'.

It is mostly from the Greek that More makes his other punning names in the narrative. The name of his traveller, Raphael, is from the Hebrew, for a change, and translates into something like 'God's physician' or 'salvation-bringer' (to the decadent Europe of More's text?). But Raphael's second name, and the one by which he is mostly called, is Hythlodaeus (Hythloday), which contradicts the supposed meaning of 'Raphael' in characteristic fashion; the Greek words for 'nonsense' and 'knowing' are combined ('learned in nonsense') to undermine any danger of our taking him seriously. Other punning names which depend on an understanding of Greek are those for various Utopian features: the island of Abraxa from the heretical invention of a heaven on earth, the town Amaurotum (Amaurote) from a word meaning 'shadowy', 'Philarch' (head of a tribe) literally meaning 'one who loves power' (ironic in the context), the river Anydrus (Anyder) more recognizably meaning 'waterless', and so on. This element of punning and of playing games with language is only partly an élitist and private or coterie thing. Readers need not be very sophisticated to see through the heavy hints in More's introductory letter to Peter Giles, with its winks and nudges about his having forgotten to ask Hythloday the exact location of so important an island, or misremembering the precise width of its principal river. The 'festive' or entertaining element in More's title allows for serious matter (if such it is) to be made palatable with lighter embellishments (to sugar the pill, so to speak). Such a convention may seem patronizing in its assumption of a wider audience, probably a gullible one, which knowing superiors may irresponsibly laugh at, thus perpetuating its exploitability, or else responsibly recognize as vulnerable, in need of protection as well as education out of superstition. Humanist concerns with the word have a strong moral and political dimension; questions of authorship, of authority, of the power of rhetoric, of the responsibilities accompanying the knowledge which brings such power, were urgent in the increasingly secular world which Erasmus and More and their fellows addressed with such anxiety that the spirit should not be lost to the letter, or the conceptual be buried beneath the material.

Whatever ideals are expressed in More's book, or lie behind it, a central paradox or contradiction is in the compromise its author has to describe between ideal and reality (though with Plato in mind, who teaches that the ideal *is* the only reality, it is less confusing to refer to the world we know as actual rather than real). The circumstances of the book's conception and composition illustrate very well More's own situation, and, beyond the particular poignancy of some aspects of his life, the un-utopian condition of human nature in general. The structure of the book makes the point, educatively for the reader, partly as a matter of deliberate shaping and partly through More's response to contingency. Circumstance determines structure, whatever the original plan may have been. It is assumed that the idea of the *Utopia* took shape in More's mind, though aspects of its theme must have long been with him, during a lull in the proceedings of a diplomatic mission in 1515. The purpose of the errand was to negotiate trading agreements with the future head of the Holy Roman Empire, Charles V, rival to the French King Francis I in a Europe where Henry VIII also had territorial ambitions. If utopia must always be essentially a dream it is appropriate for it to occur in the heads of men whose normal business is temporarily suspended and who are at the same time relieved of domestic pressures, as were More and the friends he was able to spend time with (including Peter Giles in Antwerp, to whom Erasmus recommended More ahead of More's arrival there). Something of this feeling of leisure, as well as straight literary convention for fictional romance or for academic debate, informs the framework setting of Raphael's strange story, told in a garden, on a green bench, in instalments. The 'characters' in the 'story' are the mysterious narrator Raphael and an audience of figures from real life, Peter Giles and More himself being given speaking parts. J. H. Hexter, one of the twentieth-century editors of the Yale edition of *Utopia*, worked out the accepted scheme for the composition of the book, taking account of More's prefatory letter and of the delay in time between his continental sojourn and the eventual publication of *Utopia*.

Hexter argues persuasively that the introductory account (the first six pages of our text) of the meeting of the party who are to hear Raphael's story must break off at the point where More hints at other matters to be related but then says: 'Now at this time I am determined to rehearse only that he told us of . . . the Utopians.' Some small narrative adjustments to the frame story at the end of Book I, which disguise the interruption and make credible the time span, obscure the fact that the work as first conceived ran straight on into Book II. The rest of Book I, and the conclusion at the end of Book II, where we are reminded of the debate structure out of which Raphael's long account seems to have arisen so naturally, were written after More had settled back into affairs in England. In this context the structure of the whole book, and perhaps some aspects of More's relationship with the fictional Raphael, become interdependent. Before embarking on the narrative, the reader encounters, variously selected and arranged in various editions, those prefatory letters of which the most essential is More's own to Peter Giles. Some features of this are conventional: the modest disclaimer that More has acted purely as scribe to another man's story, along with the excuses for lack of polish in the style (Raphael's Latin was not as good as his Greek), signals that the work is a fiction with devices familiar throughout literary tradition, while also acting as a personal apology for delay and inattention because of pressures on More's time (Utopia would know no such pressures). Ralph Robinson's letter in its turn, dedicating his 1551 translation to William Cecil, who was prominent in affairs of state through three reigns, is also conventional. It uses a favourite classical reference to the cynic philosopher Diogenes, thumping his tub while all about have serious work to do, for a decoratively eloquent version of the authorial apology for modest achievements; five years earlier François Rabelais, heavily influenced by the spirit of More's *Utopia*, had introduced one of his own satirical fictions with the same device, in his 'Prologue' to the *Tiers Livre* of 1546. One more feature of Robinson's letter worth mentioning is his diplomatic reference, in relation to recent history, to Thomas More's 'wilful and stubborn obstinacy' and his lament at the blindness of so great a man to 'God's holy truth in certain principal points of Christian religion'. Robinson also uses a conventional literary trick in pretending that he had to be persuaded by friends to print the book more or less against his will, and of course he bemoans, not More's inadequacies in Latin, but his own lack of skill in the vernacular which was by now developing fast as a language in which to be eloquent.

A large part of More's letter to Giles details the responsibilities and commitments that leave him no time, he complains, to write or to think. Here it is not a matter of the author protesting too much: what we have is a vivid account of More's existence at the centre of a series of concentric circles of relationships. First there is his family, where wife, children and servants all demand and deserve attention; More's domestic life was indeed important to him, including as it did the little school in which his favourite daughter Margaret first showed her considerable aptitudes. Beyond this intimate circle was that of More's professional life as a successful lawyer. Wider still was the sphere of civic activity belonging to the role of Under-Sheriff to the City of London. Within two years of the publication of *Utopia* More was to enter directly into the service of the King, and to become involved in crises which eventually lost him his freedom and his life, as he persisted in giving ultimate service to an even higher master: few men can have been more aware of difficulties in the relationship between the individual and the social self, or of that Platonic concept of justice as a harmony between micro-cosm and macrocosm. This is the man who has engaged in a fictional debate with an imaginary traveller about the duties and disadvantages of taking service at the court of a monarch. He is also the friend of Erasmus, who though courted by more than one head of state managed to avoid compromising himself, sought to transcend religious and political differences in his spirit of reform for the whole Church, and had no family ties. For all one knows, each man might have envied the other, and there are ways in which each could be seen as the other's *alter ego*. More had earlier in his career evidently been strongly drawn to the life of contemplation rather than action. He came instead into a material and affluent sphere of business and comparative power; he married (twice), and is reputed to have worn a hair shirt in secret. He also had the problem, rehearsed in the first Book of *Utopia*, of coming to terms both with the invitations of a king who might be influenced to rule wisely, if not quite as a Platonic philosopher, and with the realization that such hopes were virtually certain to be dashed in the attempt. It is a feature of the utopian tradition, named after More but not begun by him, that the author of the utopian dream has often been close to the centre of power, in a position seemingly of both trust and influence upon a ruler, yet expressing in his fiction a recognition of ultimate failure; Plato is responsible for such apparent self-defeatism – but also for the spirit that persists in valuing the enterprise of setting up models by which the real world may be measured and found wanting.

In the fiction we have not Erasmus but Raphael Hythloday, another, even freer, spirit and possible *alter ego* for Thomas More. More's prefatory letter to Giles brings Raphael out into the world of those real, substantial citizens who provide the book with testimonials, playing the game of joking seriously. There were other letters than those printed with the present text, some of them added in the quick succession of editions as the book gained in importance and popularity, along with such playful apparatus as the Utopian alphabet and poems, so that the whole gains stature as a sort of collaborative venture by a coterie of at least half a dozen leading European humanist scholars and men of affairs: councillors as well as philosophers, one might say. There is thus, for the reader, an early test of judgement and sense in the fact that real and trustworthy leaders of intellectual society (and are such as these in fact to be trusted, and if so, why?) are working on the one hand to confirm the credibility of the narrative, and on the other to undermine that assurance with broad hints at its fictionality. Governing the contribution of such items to the structure and purpose of More's book is, in fact, a process by which the reader, as the recipient of an educative if diverting experience, is led, like the philosophers leaving the cave in Plato's *Republic*, on a voyage from illusion to opinion to belief, forced to examine his progress, and finally, inevitably, denied absolute knowledge. We discover, sometimes with amusement and sometimes with dismay, what slender evidence decides our acceptance of truths or untruths. For example, More regrets a lapse of memory and an argument with a companion which disables him from being sure of the measurement of a bridge, as though the truth of the whole might be settled by a trivial statistic. The reader is prepared by this easy test for the statement that follows, More's careful signalling that there are lies *and* lies, reminding us that Raphael, the vanished, unconsultable Raphael, is in sole possession of the 'facts'. This in turn prepares us for the greater, and more ridiculously culpable (as if it mattered!) omission of Utopia's geographical location: its entire reality to be determined statistically. Again, only the missing Raphael can answer a question which is ruefully a mystery to one letter-writer after another. Meanwhile More continues to protest his anxiety to be truthful, and one of his collaborators further alerts the reader with a sympathetic marginal note, added to later editions, to a distinction between one kind of lie and another. The real purpose of all this tomfoolery is of course to educate the reader newly vulnerable to credulous acceptance of all that he is told in print, or by travellers whose tall stories he is not in a position to prove wrong. It is almost as though More were anticipating and warning against those extremes of materialistic exploitation in our secular world that make modern fools vulnerable to the glossy mailbox offer of personal eligibility for some glittering prize or time-share bargain.

But that would be only half the lesson, and everything about this text comes double-sided. The other lesson is that truth may be more potent, as well as more palatable, when presented in fictional guise. Both lessons, or their interdependence, owe much in More's understanding of them to the stimulating example of the satirist Lucian, some of whose work More and Erasmus delightedly translated, and whose *True History* suggests that its own title is a contradiction in terms, while teasing the reader by obliging him to believe first nothing and then everything he is told, to distrust the narrator and yet to waste time questioning the validity of the blatantly spurious statistics offered. The relationship between truth and belief-worthiness (not credibility) is a complex one; the 'utopian' truth that certain natural human weaknesses and vices necessitate social control, for example, justifies Plato's Myth of the Metals (taken up negatively in *Brave New World* where individuals must accept their predetermined status, from Alpha to Epsilon, in their own interests as well as society's). The same argument allows an element of myth or fiction in Christian doctrine, against the dangers of literal-minded fundamentalism, showing the necessity for such devices as allegory and parable to make truths accessible which would otherwise defeat human powers of comprehension. That More is looking for an open-minded reader, sceptical in that positive human-

istic sense which uses more sophisticated measures than facts
or statistics, is clear from the last portion of his letter to Giles,
in which he practically invents his own reader, one who will
heed the string of disqualifications, learning good habits by
dissociating himself from bad ones. This passage may be
likened to the obviously conventional 'modesty' of translator
Robinson's introduction, but may also be seen to go far beyond
it; it has, in fact, more than a little in common with the
protests made to Martin Dorp, that earlier unsympathetic
reader of Erasmus's *Praise of Folly*.

Educative procedures multiply as the text gets under way,
for telling, showing, demonstrating and arguing has each its
place. One device by which More suggests his meaning is that
of literary allusion. If Raphael is a kind of *alter ego* – for either
his views oppose those of the narrative figure called More
(who may not be the real-life More), or they are More's private
beliefs, delivered discreetly through another's mouth – then
the way he is introduced is significant. The meeting echoes
features from the opening of Plato's *Republic*, where a group
coming away from religious devotions similarly encounters,
and learns the characteristics of, the parties to the debate that
is to follow. Plato's Thrasymachus uses force of numbers to
persuade, so that Socrates' company may learn about dialectic
methods. More discovers a traveller, whose credentials come
from the mouth of Peter Giles himself, now also a narrative
participant. The significant things about Raphael are that,
looking much travelled, almost wild, he has been with Vespucci
(the account of whose voyages was recently in print) to America
and other remote territories; but, to balance the spuriously
credible associations with real life, Raphael also resembles
first Ulysses and then Plato himself. From Plato presumably
comes his philosophic temper (though he later proves fairly
excitable), and the experience or imagination to describe an
ideal society; with regard to the question of service as a
counsellor, as it later develops, Plato had of course not only
travelled but had attempted the guidance and education of
the tyrant Dionysius of Syracuse. Ulysses, on the other hand,
is a poetic model, the archetypal traveller and adventurer,
original of the hero as pragmatic opportunist, but also carrying

the concept of the hero whose prime duty is to find his way home and govern his land justly. Raphael, we are aware, has not settled at home, but wandered off (irresponsibly, like some post-Homeric Ulysses?) as More, after his own brief sortie abroad, was poignantly unable to do. Moreover Raphael has abnegated all social roles. It is Peter Giles, not More, who first introduces the theme of service, of the use that Raphael's experiences might be to the governor of a society, and who elicits the information that Raphael has in effect bought his freedom from domestic commitments and thinks it hardly matters where he dies. The quasi-Platonic debate that follows, with More and Peter together questioning Raphael, is generally called the Dialogue of Council, and whatever relevance it might have to the humanist lawyer and citizen, it is Raphael's experiences which, he insists, would hardly be listened to by any European king, while More and Peter try to convince him of a social duty.

Brief and tantalizing sketches of fictional societies superior to those of Europe precede the account of Utopia (reserved for Book II), while the extended account of the current state of England provides a reasoned critique of an unjust and corrupt society, verifiable by experience for an English reader of the time (or even since), in such a way as to render more emotionally irresistible and *educationally desirable* the reforming fiction of Utopia when it finally comes. Excuses for not serving or advising at court consist of some fairly savage observations of kings whose habits fall short of the Platonic ideal – but such criticisms are tactfully, that is, satirically, aimed at France rather than England. A striking narrative device, which partly distances the debate from More, and partly involves him even more closely, is the introduction of a further dialogue within the Dialogue, this time a reported account of an occasion when Raphael claims to have been at the house of Cardinal Morton, patron, employer and mentor to More in his childhood. Here another small company of debaters rehearses, dramatically, the operation of prejudices that Raphael says would make his service to a king quite useless in actuality. A complacent lawyer and an incontinent friar are among the caricatured personifications of bias, while the figure of Cardinal Morton listens, placates, modifies and is diffident in expressing opinions. There is surely something decisive for More personally in his presentation of this powerful figure, for the Cardinal has influence by virtue of his power and position, without being corrupted by either, and he offers a sounder model for More himself than do the in-some-ways enviable life and freedoms of Raphael. Raphael's privileges, one notes, include the freedom to speak, demonstrated most fiercely in his peroration at the end of Book II, where his diatribe against pride is the climax of More's book.

The occasion at Cardinal Morton's shows a figure of authority exercising his influence modestly, even if he is respected for the wrong reasons. Clever, impassioned, flippant and abusive speeches have brought no resolution, but only run throuh the gamut of rhetorical poses. Yet when the Cardinal shows himself truly interested in the hypothetical *possibility* of Raphael's social amendments, suddenly 'every man gave great praise to my sayings, which a little before they had disallowed. But most of all was esteemed that which was ... the cardinal's own addition.' It is after this glimpse of a great figure using his influence as well as circumstances will allow that the narrative returns to the frame of the outer dialogue, where the discussion of the value of the counsellor's role comes to its conclusion in More's own suggestion that the philosopher has a responsibility to do the best that worldly circumstances will permit: not to compromise, but to adapt.

This may seem to suggest a role for Raphael which is indeed closely related to a familiar view of Book I as centred on an inner dialogue in which More considers his own part in public life. Such a view has to be tested by readers, as does every other feature of the narrative and its structure, a wealth of experience through reading not to be described or summarized here. To suggest an interpretation is not to prescribe one, and the latter act would be perversely out of sympathy with the spirit of More's book and of the traditions, literary, philosophical, rhetorical, which express that spirit. There are many teasing moments in Book II where a reader knowing something of the real-life opinions and temperament of Thomas More, and knowing too that More is aiming to persuade an imagined reader, will not know what to make of certain Utopian customs, or whether More would approve his own inventions. This is not a book which tells us what to think, but rather that it is necessary to think. More's final paragraph is of course the final test, or opportunity. Raphael has had his say, absolute and uncompromising as he might justifiably be in his attack on pride. More re-enters the field in a tone which is judiciously anticlimactic, one might say, as though practising that cautious, understated adaptation to the circumstances of the real world which the writing of the narrative has taught him – his own first pupil. It is a paragraph of the most subtle doubleness, of vision and of appeal. It is full of reservations, caveats, open-ended interest – and apparently dismissive certainties. Truth, and value, are available only through the medium of words; the most prominent words here are those expressing the concepts of 'nobility, magnificence, worship, honour, and majesty'. It is in 'the common opinion' that these are 'the true ornaments and honours ... of a commonwealth'. All the reader has to do is to sort out the distinction between ideal abstractions and earthly adaptations, compromises, corruptions, abuses and misuses, resolve (not reduce) complexity into simplicity, and then reform 'the common opinion' which all humanity must share!

Jenny Mezciems

SELECT BIBLIOGRAPHY

Thomas More's works are being collected in sixteen volumes in *The Yale Edition of the Complete Works of St Thomas More*, Yale University Press, New Haven and London. Volume IV, *Utopia*, ed. Edward Surtz, S. J., and J. H. Hexter (1965), is based on the Latin text of the 1518 Basle edition, with facing pages carrying the 1923 English translation by G. C. Richards. This invaluable volume has a 194-page introduction as well as some 320 pages of scholarly notes and commentary. A smaller Yale series of Selected Works makes the *Utopia* available in paperback, with modern spelling and a more modest commentary, edited by Edward Surtz, S. J. (1964). In the same series, but not reprinted lately, is the *Selected Letters*, ed. Elizabeth Frances Rogers (1961), which prints letters to Erasmus and the one to Dorp of 1515.

OTHER NOTEWORTHY EDITIONS

Libellus vere aureus nec minus salutaris quam festivus de optimo reipublicae statu, deque nova Insula Utopia, Martens, Louvain, 1516.
De Optimo reipublicae statu, deque nova insula Utopia . . ., G. de Gourmont, Paris, 1517.
De optimo reipublicae statu, deque nova insula Utopia . . ., J. Froben, Basle, 1518.
A fruteful and pleasaunt worke of the beste state of a publyque weale, and of the newe yle called Utopia, translated into English by Raphe Robynson, A. Vele, London, 1551.
Utopia, ed. William Morris, Kelmscott Press, 1893. Robinson's text.
Utopia, ed. J. H. Lupton, Clarendon Press, 1895. The Latin text with Robinson's translation.
Utopia, trans. Paul Turner, Penguin, 1965. Attractive modern translation, with introduction and notes.
Utopia, trans. Robert M. Adams, W. W. Norton, New York and London, 1976. Critical Edition, with selected essays.

RELATED TEXTS AND SECONDARY MATERIAL (BOOKS AND ARTICLES)

ADAMS, ROBERT P., *The Better Part of Valor: More, Erasmus, Colet, and Vives, on Humanism, War, and Peace, 1496–1535*, University of Washington Press, Seattle, 1962. On humanist pacificism.
AMES, RUSSELL A., *Citizen Thomas More and His Utopia*, Princeton University Press, Princeton, N.J., 1949. Still worth reading for More as Republican; compare Kautsky (below) on More as Marxist.

SELECT BIBLIOGRAPHY

AUGUSTINE, SAINT, *The City of God*, trans. John Healey, ed. R. G. V. Tasker, Dent, 1957.

BAKER-SMITH, DOMINIC, *More's 'Utopia'*, Unwin Critical Library, London and New York: HarperCollins Academic, 1991. A balanced and scholarly study of text and background.

BERGER, HARRY, JR, 'The Renaissance Imagination: Second World and Green World', *Centennial Review of Arts and Sciences*, 9 (1965), 36–78.

BEVINGTON, DAVID, 'The Dialogue in *Utopia*: Two Sides to the Question', *Studies in Philology*, 58 (1961), 496–509. On the authorial ambiguities.

BOLT, ROBERT, *A Man for All Seasons*, Random House, New York, 1960; Heinemann, London, 10496041. Popular and influential play, twice filmed.

CHAMBERS, R. W., *Thomas More*, Jonathan Cape, 1935; reprinted Penguin, 1963. Once the standard biography, with emphasis on More as a saint.

DAVIS, J. C., *Utopia and the Ideal Society: A Study of English Utopian Writing, 1516–1700*, Cambridge University Press, 1981. Useful for its definitions and categories.

ELIAV-FELDON, MIRIAM, *Realistic Utopias: The Ideal Imaginary Societies of the Renaissance, 1516–1630*, Clarendon Press, 1982.

ELLIOTT, ROBERT C., *The Shape of Utopia: Studies in a Literary Genre*, University of Chicago Press, Chicago and London, 1970.

ERASMUS, *The Praise of Folly*, trans. Betty Radice, Penguin, 1971.

ERASMUS, *The Praise of Folly*, trans. Clarence H. Miller, Yale University Press, New Haven and London, 1979. Includes the Letter to Dorp.

FOX, ALISTAIR, *Thomas More: History and Providence*, Basil Blackwell, 1982; Yale University Press, New Haven and London, 1983. One of the major biographies.

FOX, ALISTAIR, and GUY, JOHN, *Reassessing the Henrician Age: Humanism, Politics and Reform, 1500–1550*, Basil Blackwell, 1986.

GILL, CHRISTOPHER, 'Plato's Atlantis Story and the Birth of Fiction', *Philosophy and Literature*, 3 (1979), 64–78.

GUY, JOHN, *The Public Career of Sir Thomas More*, Harvester Press, 1980.

HEISERMAN, A. R., 'Satire in the *Utopia*', *Publications of the Modern Language Association of America*, 78 (1963), 163–74.

HEXTER, J. H., *More's 'Utopia': The Biography of an Idea*, Princeton University Press, Princeton, N.J., 1952; reprinted with new 'Epilogue', Harper Torchbooks, Harper and Row, New York, 1965. Influential account of the book's composition.

HEXTER, J. H., 'Thomas More and the Problem of Counsel', *Albion*, 10, Supplement (1978), 55–66. This volume is a Quincentennial collection, including essays by, e.g., Thomas I. White and Warren W. Wooden.

UTOPIA

HOGREFE, PEARL, *The Sir Thomas More Circle*, University of Illinois Press, Urbana, 1959.

JOHNSON, R. S., *More's 'Utopia': Ideal and Illusion*, Yale University Press, New Haven and London, 1969.

JONES, EMRYS, 'Commoners and Kings: Book One of More's *Utopia*', in *Medieval Studies for J. A. W. Bennett*, ed. P. L. Heyworth, Clarendon Press, 1981, pp. 255–72.

JONES, JUDITH, *Thomas More*, Twayne's English Authors, G. K. Hall, Boston, Mass., 1979. Useful introductory survey of the life and works.

KAUTSKY, KARL, *Thomas More and His 'Utopia'*, trans. H. J. Stenning, A & C Black, 1927. A once famously controversial Marxist reading.

KENNEDY, WILLIAM J., *Rhetorical Norms in Renaissance Literature*, Yale University Press, New Haven and London, 1978. Extremely useful introductory study of rhetoric.

KRISTELLER, P. O., *Renaissance Thought and Its Sources*, ed. Michael Mooney, Columbia University Press, New York, 1979.

LOGAN, GEORGE M., *The Meaning of More's 'Utopia'*, Princeton University Press, Princeton, N.J., 1983. Useful on sources.

LUCIAN, *Satirical Sketches*, trans. Paul Turner, Penguin, 1961.

LUCIAN, *Selected Satires*, trans. Lionel Casson, W. W. Norton, New York and London, 1968.

MANUEL, FRANK E., and FRITZIE P., *Utopian Thought in the Western World*, Basil Blackwell, 1979.

MARIUS, RICHARD, *Thomas More: A Biography*, Knopf, New York, 1984; Dent, London, 1985.

MCCUTCHEON, ELIZABETH, *My Dear Peter: The Ars Poetica and Hermeneutics of More's 'Utopia'*, Moreana, Angers, 1983. Valuable account of the function of the letters.

MEZCIEMS, JENNY, 'Utopia and "the Thing which is not": More, Swift, and Other Lying Idealists', *University of Toronto Quarterly*, 52 (1982), 40–62.

Miscellanea Moreana: Essays for Germain Marc'hadour, ed. Clare M. Murphy and others, Medieval and Renaissance Texts and Studies, Binghampton, 1989. Several essays on *Utopia*.

NAGEL, ALAN F., 'Lies and the Limitable Inane: Contradiction in More's *Utopia*', *Renaissance Quarterly*, 26 (1973), 173–80.

PLATO, *The Republic*, trans. Desmond Lee, Penguin, 1955; revised 1974. Good notes and commentary.

RAITIERE, MARTIN N., 'More's *Utopia* and *The City of God*', *Studies in the Renaissance*, 20 (1973), 144–68. An important source considered.

ROPER, WILLIAM, *The Lyfe of Sir Thomas More, Knighte*, ed. E. V. Hitchcock, Early English Text Society, Oxford University Press, 1935. The first biography (1550s), by More's son-in-law; published 1626.

SELECT BIBLIOGRAPHY

St Thomas More: Action and Contemplation, ed. Richard Sylvester, Yale University Press, New Haven, 1972. Four good essays, from 1970 Symposium at St John's University.

SURTZ, EDWARD, S. J., *The Praise of Pleasure*, Harvard University Press, Cambridge, Mass., 1957, and *The Praise of Wisdom*, Loyola University Press, Chicago, 1957. Important Catholic readings of the man and the works.

Twentieth Century Interpretations of 'Utopia': A Collection of Critical Essays, ed. William Nelson, Prentice-Hall, Englewood Cliffs, N.J., 1968. Selection of reprinted essays, useful for students.

WEINER, ANDREW D., 'Raphael's Eutopia and More's *Utopia*; Christian Humanism and the Limits of Reason', *Huntington Library Quarterly*, 39 (1975/76), 1–27.

CHRONOLOGY

DATE	AUTHOR'S LIFE	LITERARY CONTEXT
1474–7		
1477 or 1478	Thomas More born in Milk Street in the Cripplegate ward of the City of London (7 February), the son of John More, a successful lawyer who was to become a knight and a justice of the King's Bench, and Agnes, née Graunger.	
1482		Marsilio Ficino's Latin translation of Plato.
1483		
1485	Begins attending St Anthony's Grammar School in Threadneedle Street.	
1486		Pico della Mirandola: *De dignitate hominis*.
1490	Page in the household of John Morton, Archbishop of Canterbury and Lord Chancellor.	
1491		
1492–4	Studies at Oxford University (Canterbury College). Writing poetry in English and Latin.	
1492–1504		
1494	Leaves Oxford without acquiring a degree; enrols as a Law student at New Inn. Continues Latin studies privately.	
1496	Enters Lincoln's Inn.	
1497	First Latin verses published in John Holt's Latin grammar, *Lac puerorum*.	
1497–8		

Caxton prints his first book in Bruges (1474); sets up a press at Westminster (1476); prints first book in England (1477).
Duke of Clarence murdered in the Tower (1478).

Death of Edward IV. Richard, Duke of Gloucester, becomes first Protector, afterwards king; Edward V deposed and murdered.
Battle of Bosworth Field: Henry VII becomes first Tudor king. Yeomen of the Guard established.

Henry marries Elizabeth of York, daughter of Edward IV.

1490s: Savonarola preaching in Florence.

William Grocyn at Exeter College, Oxford; introduces first lectures in Greek at the university.
Death of Lorenzo de' Medici (1492).

Columbus and Vespucci reach West Indies and America.
Charles VIII of France invades Italy and takes Rome. Aldo Manuzio establishes Aldine Press in Venice. Paper manufacture in England.

John Colet, lecturing on the Epistles of St Paul at Oxford, brings Christian humanism to England. Leonardo painting *The Last Supper*. John Cabot, under the patronage of Henry VII, sails across the Atlantic to Cape Breton Island.

DATE	AUTHOR'S LIFE	LITERARY CONTEXT
1499	Meets Erasmus, visiting London for the first time. Presents verses to the young Prince Henry (future Henry VIII).	(c.) Skelton: *The Bowge of Court*.
1500	In spite of his youth, More already associated with a circle of eminent humanist scholars including Thomas Linacre and William Grocyn (under whose aegis he was learning Greek), John Colet and William Lily.	Erasmus's first collection of classical proverbs, *Collectanea Adagiorum*.
1501	Called to the Bar. About this time, Lily and More begin translating epigrams from the *Greek Anthology* into Latin (not published until 1518).	
1501–4	Lives in partial retreat in the Charterhouse (possibly testing a vocation for the priesthood). Teaches Law at Furnivall's Inn. Lectures on St Augustine's *City of God* (c. 1501) at St Lawrence Jewry. Translating a Latin life of Pico della Mirandola.	
1503	Composes elegy on the death of Elizabeth of York.	Erasmus: *Enchiridion Militis Christiani* (*Handbook of a Christian Knight*). William Dunbar: *The Thissil and the Ros*.
c. 1503–7		Vespucci: *Mundus Novus* (various editions of the *Voyages*).
1505	Marries Jane Colt, daughter of an Essex gentleman farmer, who will bear him four children (Margaret, Elizabeth, Cecily and John). Sets up home in Bucklersbury, off Cheapside.	Birth of poet Thomas Wyatt.
1505–6	Erasmus's second visit to England. More works with him at translating Lucian's satires from Greek into Latin (published in Paris, 1506).	
1508	Journeys to the Continent (Louvain and Paris).	Erasmus's expanded *Adagia* becomes the world's first bestseller.

CHRONOLOGY

Execution of Perkin Warbeck, pretender to the English throne.

By 1500 estimated to be 17,000 printing presses in operation throughout Europe. Wynkyn de Worde establishes press in Fleet Street – its first connection with the printing industry.

Marriage of Catherine of Aragon with Arthur, Prince of Wales, who dies the following year.

Death of Elizabeth of York. Formal betrothal of Catherine of Aragon to twelve-year-old Prince Henry. Marriage of Princess Margaret, eldest daughter of Henry VII, to James IV of Scotland. Giuliano della Rovere becomes Pope as Julius II (to 1513): patron of Bramante, Michelangelo, Raphael.

Leonardo: *La Gioconda* (the *Mona Lisa*).

Michelangelo begins painting the ceiling of the Sistine Chapel. In his campaign to restore the Papal States, Julius II conquers Perugia and Bologna.

DATE	AUTHOR'S LIFE	LITERARY CONTEXT
1509	Erasmus stays with the Mores in Bucklersbury, where he writes *The Praise of Folly*. More building up a large and successful practice as a barrister; also made a Bencher at Lincoln's Inn. Becomes a freeman of the Mercers' Company. Elected to Parliament, as one of the four members for Westminster (December).	Sebastian Brant's *Das Narrenschift* (1494) translated by Alexander Barclay as *The Ship of Fools*. (c.) *Everyman* (morality play).
1510	Attends House of Commons for the January–February session. Publication of More's *Life of John Picus, Earl of Mirandola*. Becomes Under-Sheriff of London (to 1518).	
1511	Death of his wife, Jane. More remarries Alice Middleton, widow of a London mercer. Reader at Lincoln's Inn.	Erasmus: *Moriae Enconium* (*The Praise of Folly*). Peter Martyr d'Anghiera: *De orbe novo* (Columbus's records).
1511–14	Family 'school' established: More's children, various wards, and later his grandchildren are educated at home, following a humanist curriculum devised by More himself.	
1512		Erasmus: *De ratione studii* (a study of language).
1513	Starts writing his unfinished *History of King Richard III*. Composes verses celebrating Henry VIII's French expedition.	Machiavelli: *Il principe* (published 1532). John Skelton: *The Ballade of the Scottysshe Kynge*. *De constructione*, Lily and Erasmus's Latin grammar prepared for Colet's school.
1514	Admitted to Doctors' Commons. Teaching grammar at Oxford.	Barclay: (c.) *Eclogues*.
1515	More sent on diplomatic mission to Flanders. Friendship with Peter Giles begins in Antwerp. Becomes Senior Reader at Lincoln's Inn.	Skelton: *Magnificence* (morality play).
1516	*Utopia* completed and published in Louvain. More joins his father and Colet as a member of the King's council, which is controlled by Wolsey.	Erasmus: *Institutio Christiani Principis* (*The Education of a Christian Prince*); Greek New Testament (published at Basle); *Colloquia* (first of several editions).

CHRONOLOGY

John Colet founds St Paul's School in London (opens 1512, with Lily as first high master). Henry VIII crowned; marries Catherine of Aragon. League of Cambrai: defeat of Venice; Papal States restored to Pope.

Henry VIII joins Holy League against France. St John's College, Cambridge, founded under the auspices of John Fisher, Bishop of Rochester.

Erasmus lecturing on Greek in Cambridge, and working on his New Testament.

Julius II convenes Fifth Lateran Council. The French driven from northern Italy.
Henry VIII invades France. English army defeats the Scots at Flodden: James IV is killed. Edmund de la Pole, chief Yorkist claimant to the English throne, executed for alleged treason.

Peace with France. Princess Mary (Henry VIII's younger sister) marries Louis XII of France but is widowed eleven weeks later. Work begins on Thomas Wolsey's Hampton Court.
Accession of Francis I in France. French invade northern Italy and regain control of Milan. Wolsey is made a Cardinal (September); becomes Lord Chancellor (December).

Birth of Princess Mary, future Queen Mary I. French Concordat with Leo X. Richard Fox establishes Corpus Christi, Oxford.

DATE	AUTHOR'S LIFE	LITERARY CONTEXT
1516 cont		Ariosto: *Orlando Furioso*. Birth of poet Henry Howard, Earl of Surrey.
1517	Embassy to Calais. *Utopia* printed in Paris. During Mayday riots, More one of the officials who attempts – unsuccessfully – to persuade the mob to disperse.	Erasmus: *Querela pacis* (*The Complaint of Peace*). Skelton: *The Tunnyng of Elynour Rummyng*.
1518	*Utopia* printed in Basle, together with More's *Epigrammata* (Latin poems). More made councillor attendant and *de facto* a member of the Privy Chamber.	Machiavelli: *Mandragola*.
1519		Machiavelli: *Discorsi* (published 1531).
*c.*1519 – *c.*1521		Vives: *In Pseudo-dialecticos* (anti-obscurantist). Skelton: *Collyn Clout*; *Speke Parrot*. John Rastell (More's brother-in-law, a lawyer, printer and playwright): *A New Interlude and a Merry of the IIII Elements*.
1520	More is present at the Field of the Cloth of Gold; meets Guillaume Budé, French humanist. Journeys to Bruges to resolve disputes with the Hanse merchants. New edition of *Epigrammata* includes a verse epistle to his children.	Luther: *An Appeal to the Christian Nobility of the German Nation*; *Concerning the Babylonish Captivity of the Church*; *On the Liberty of a Christian Man*. Germanius de Brie ('Brixius'): *Antimorus* (attack on More).
1521	More is knighted. Becomes Under-Treasurer. Travels to Bruges with Wolsey for secret negotiations with Charles V.	Henry VIII: *Assertio septem Sacramentorum adversus Martin Lutherum* (treatise in defence of the Seven Sacraments).
1522	Writes treatise *The Four Last Things* (published 1557). Delivers oration on treaty with Charles V.	Skelton: (*c.*) *Why Come Ye Nat to Court*. Tunstall: *De arte supputandi* (treatise on arithmetic, dedicated to More).
1523	Elected Speaker of the House of Commons. Publishes the *Responsio ad Lutherum*, in reply to Luther's diatribe against Henry VIII.	Skelton: *The Garlande of Laurell*.

HISTORICAL EVENTS

Evil Mayday riot: mob of London apprentices attack foreign merchants in the City – riot suppressed and eleven hanged. The Fifth Lateran Council closes without having achieved any major reform of the Church. Luther's ninety-five theses published at Wittenberg. Wolsey announces the creation of six new professorships at Oxford.
Thomas Linacre founds Royal College of Physicians.

Charles V elected Holy Roman Emperor after the death of Emperor Maximilian. Magellan embarks on voyage round the world (to 1522).

Charles V visits England. Henry VIII and Francis I meet at the Field of the Cloth of Gold. Francis I founds the Royal Library, Paris (later the Bibliothèque Nationale).

Henry VIII made Defender of the Faith. Diet of Worms: Luther condemned. In England, his books burned. Execution of Edward, Duke of Buckingham, on a charge of treason.

Luther's German translation of the New Testament. Henry VIII declares war on France and Scotland. Charles V in England: Treaty of Windsor.

Imperial and English forces invade France; Duke of Suffolk's army within seventy miles of Paris but obliged to retreat. Clement VII becomes Pope. Zwingli reforms Zurich. Spanish humanist Juan Luis Vives in England (to 1527): lectures in Greek at Oxford (probably due to More's influence) and becomes tutor to Princess Mary.

DATE	AUTHOR'S LIFE	LITERARY CONTEXT
1524	Having completed his duties as Speaker, resumes his role as the King's secretary and adviser. Appointed High Steward of Oxford University.	Erasmus: *De libero arbitrio* (*On Free Will* – in opposition to Luther) and final edition of the *Colloquia*. Luther's German Hymnbook. Vives: *Introductio ad Sapientam* (*An Introduction to Wisdom*); *De institutione feminae Christianae* (*On the Education of a Christian Woman*) – More commissions an English translation from Richard Hyrde.
1525	Appointed Chancellor of the Duchy of Lancaster. High Steward of Cambridge University. Entrusted with secret negotiations for a truce with France. Writes unpublished reply to Bugenhagen.	Luther: *De servo arbitrio* (in response to Erasmus). John Bugenhagen: *Letter to the English* (Lutheran tract). Zwingli: *Commentarius de vera et de falsa religione.*
1525/6	About this time, More's new house in Chelsea is completed, and the family moves in. Rastell publishes two humorous works from the More household: *The Twelve Mery Jests of Wyddow Edyth* and *A Hundred Merry Tales*. More becoming closely involved with the detection of heresy in London and the Universities.	Rastell: *Calisto and Melebea*, an interlude (*c.* 1525).
1527	Hans Holbein the Younger paints portraits of More's family. Tunstall, Bishop of London, commissions him to read and respond to heretical literature. In France for ratification of treaty of alliance.	
1528		Castiglione: *Il libro del cortegiano* (*The Book of the Courtier*) (English translation 1561). Erasmus: *Ciceronianus.* Tyndale: *Parable of the Wicked Mammon.* Tyndale's *The Obedience of a Christian Man* and Simon Fish's *Supplication for the Beggars* argue that the King should extend his authority over the Church.

HISTORICAL EVENTS

Peasants' War in Germany (to 1525).

Tyndale's English New Testament published in Cologne and Worms. It soon reaches London and is distributed privately, in spite of the efforts of Cuthbert Tunstall, Bishop of London, who issues a 'monition' against it in 1526, after which the first copies are burned. Wolsey founds Cardinal College (later Christ Church), Oxford. Charles V defeats French at Pavia, gaining control of Italy.
John Taverner appointed organist at Cardinal College, where he composes most of his church music (to 1530).

Henry VIII makes alliance with Francis I against Charles V. Sack of Rome by imperial army. Henry VIII makes first unsuccessful application to the Pope for the annulment of his marriage to Catherine of Aragon. Reformation in Sweden.

France and England declare war on Charles V. Wolsey sends deputation to Rome and secures papal agreement that the validity of the King's marriage should be decided by a legatine court in England, presided over by Cardinal Campeggio and Wolsey himself. Reformation in Basle and Berne; Bucer reforms Strassburg.

DATE	AUTHOR'S LIFE	LITERARY CONTEXT
1529	Attends peace conference at Cambrai with Tunstall, and succeeds in negotiating satisfactory terms for England. Appointed Lord Chancellor (October), in spite of his opposition to the annulment of the King's marriage. Publishes *A Dialogue concerning Heresies*, mainly directed against Tyndale's writings. Writes *Supplication of Souls* in reply to Simon Fish's treatise of the previous year. Supports measures to remedy abuses within the Church during anticlerical backlash following Wolsey's downfall. Instrumental in introducing reform of the Star Chamber.	Budé: *Commentarii linguae graecae.* Rastell: (*c.*) *The Pastyme of People, the Chronicles of dyvers Realmys and most specially of the Realme of England.*
1530	Active in both Star Chamber and Courts of Chancery. Continues to support Aragonese faction; his name significantly absent from a petition of nobles and prelates to the Pope, in favour of annulment of the King's marriage. Death of Sir John Moore.	Wynkyn de Worde: *Song Book.* Zwingli: *De providentia Dei*; *Fideo ratio.* Tyndale: *The Practice of Prelates.* Christopher St German: *Doctor and Student* (legal theorist asserts claims of common law over canon law; he is swiftly drafted onto the King's council).
1531	More obliged to announce to the House of Lords the verdict of the Universities in favour of annulment. Much engaged in the prosecution of heretics.	Sir Thomas Elyot: *The Book of the Governour.* Tyndale: *An Answer to Sir Thomas More.* Vives: *De disciplinis libri xx* (treatise on educational methods).
1532	Struggle for power with Thomas Cromwell: openly resists King's attempts to transfer powers of Church to Parliament. Resigns Chancellorship, his position untenable. First part of his *Confutation of Tyndale's Answer* appears (second part 1533).	Rabelais: *Pantagruel.* John Calvin publishes his first work, a commentary on Seneca's *De Clementia.*

CHRONOLOGY

Legatine Court sits for two months, until, in response to the Queen's demands for justice, Clement VII orders the hearing to adjourn to Rome – a deathblow to Henry's expectations. Wolsey dismissed in disgrace, and More appointed Lord Chancellor, the first layman for a hundred years to hold this position. Treaty of Cambrai: Francis I and Charles V make peace. Reformation Parliament opens. Siege of Vienna by the Turks.

Wolsey arrested as a traitor; dies on his way to London. Tyndale's English version of the Pentateuch. Persecution of reformers: royal proclamation issued for the suppppression of Tyndale's and other heretical books. Thomas Hitton burned – first Protestant martyr of the English Reformation. Diet of Augsburg presented with Lutheran confession. Charles V last Holy Roman Emperor to be crowned by the Pope.

Many more Protestant martyrs sent to the stake. Clergy pay £100,000 for having recognized Wolsey as papal legate and thus breaching the Statute of Praemunire (1351). Convocation recognizes Henry VIII as 'Supreme Head' of English Church 'as far as the Law of Christ allows'. Rise of Thomas Cromwell. Battle of Kappel and death of Zwingli.

'Supplication against the Ordinaries': Commons address Henry VIII against the authority of Church courts. Submission of the Clergy: no ecclesiastical laws without royal approval. Resignation of More; replaced by Sir Thomas Audley. Death of William Warham, Archbishop of Canterbury. Building of St James's Palace begins. Religious Peace of Nürnberg. Inquisition first established at Lisbon.

DATE	AUTHOR'S LIFE	LITERARY CONTEXT
1533	In retirement at Chelsea. Continues to oppose Cromwell's policies, engaging in a polemical battle with St German (as in *The Apology of Sir Thomas More* and *Debellation of Salem and Bizance*). Declines to attend coronation of Anne Boleyn. Under increasing surveillance.	John Heywood (playwright married to More's niece): *The Play of the Wether; A Play of Love; Witty and Witless; The Pardoner, the Frere, the Curate, and Neighbour Pratte* (interlude).
1534	Writes *A Treatise on the Passion*. Charged with treasonable association with Elizabeth Barton; proved innocent and discharged. Though expressing himself willing to subscribe to the Act of Succession, More refuses to take the oath of allegiance because it impugns the spiritual authority of the Pope: he is committed to the Tower (April), where he writes his *Dialogue of Comfort against Tribulation*.	Rabelais: *Gargantua*.
1535	Called upon to acknowledge Royal Supremacy and refuses (April). Charged with maliciously attempting to deprive Henry VIII of his title of Supreme Head of the Church in England (June). Tried (1 July) and condemned to be hanged, drawn and quartered. The King commutes the sentence to beheading. More is executed on 6 July.	Erasmus: *Ecclesiastes* (treatise on preaching).
1536		Calvin: *Christianae religionis Institutio*.
1551	First English translation of *Utopia* by Ralph Robinson (revised 1556).	
1626	Life of Thomas More by his son-in-law William Roper published in Paris.	
1886	More is beatified by the Church of Rome.	
1935	More is canonized.	

HISTORICAL EVENTS

Thomas Cranmer appointed Archbishop of Canterbury. Act in Restraint of Appeals signals break with Rome. Cranmer grants annulment of the King's marriage to Catherine of Aragon, and marries him to Anne Boleyn. Henry excommunicated by Pope Clement VII. Birth of Princess Elizabeth, future Queen Elizabeth I.

In March, the Pope pronounces Henry's marriage with Catherine valid, while the English Parliament passes Act of Succession in favour of Anne Boleyn's issue and requiring an oath of allegiance from peers, MPs and clergy. Elizabeth Barton ('the Nun of Kent') executed for prophesying against the King. Act of Supremacy confirms Henry VIII as Supreme Head of the Church. Reorganization of the friars under the King's authority: a prelude to suppression of the Order. Ignatius Loyola founds Society of Jesus. Death of Clement VII, succeeded by Paul III.

Execution of Bishop Fisher and Sir Thomas More. Cromwell forbids study of canon law at English universities. Valor Ecclesiasticus: official returns made of value of all Church lands. Coverdale's Bible: first authorized translation.

Death of Catherine of Aragon. Anne Boleyn accused of treasonable adultery and executed. Marriage of Henry VIII to Jane Seymour. Act of Succession excludes Mary and Elizabeth. Dissolution of the Monasteries begins. Tyndale, at the instigation of Henry VIII, burnt at the stake at Vilvorde, near Brussels. Death of Erasmus.

A fruteful/

and pleasaunt worke of the
beste state of a publyque weale, and
of the newe yle called Utopia: written
in Latine by Syr Thomas More
knyght, and translated into Englyshe
by Raphe Robynson Citizein and
Goldsmythe of London, at the
procurement, and earnest re=
quest of George Tadlowe
Citezein and Haberdassher
of the same Citie.

(.·.)

¶ Emprinted at London
by Abraham Uele, dwelling in Pauls
churcheyarde at the sygne of
the Lambe. Anno,

1 5 5 1.

Title page of first English edition, 1551

TO THE RIGHT HONOURABLE, AND HIS VERY
SINGULAR GOOD MASTER,

MASTER WILLIAM CECIL,
ESQUIRE,

ONE OF THE TWO PRINCIPAL SECRETARIES TO THE
KING'S MOST EXCELLENT MAJESTY,

RALPH ROBINSON WISHETH CONTINUANCE OF
HEALTH WITH DAILY INCREASE OF
VIRTUE AND HONOUR

UPON a time when tidings came to the City of Corinth
that King Philip, father to Alexander surnamed the Great,
was coming thitherward with an army royal to lay siege
to the city, the Corinthians being forthwith stricken with
great fear, began busily and earnestly to look about them
and to fall to work on all hands. Some to scour and trim
up harness, some to carry stones, some to amend and
build higher the walls, some to rampiere and fortify the
bulwarks and fortresses, some one thing and some another
for the defending and strengthening of the city. The
which busy labour and toil of theirs when Diogenes the
philosopher saw, having no profitable business where-
upon to set himself on work (neither any man required
his labour and help as expedient for the commonwealth
in that necessity), immediately girded about him his
philosophical cloak, and began to roll and tumble up and
down hither and thither upon the hillside that lieth
adjoining to the city his great barrel or tun, wherein he
dwelled, for other dwelling-place would he have none.
This seeing one of his friends, and not a little musing
thereat, came to him: and, I pray thee, Diogenes, quoth
he, why dost thou thus, or what meanest thou hereby?
Forsooth I am tumbling my tub too, quoth he, because it
were no reason that I only should be idle, where so many
be working. In semblable manner, right honourable sir,

though I be, as I am indeed, of much less ability than Diogenes was to do anything that shall or may be for the advancement and commodity of the public wealth of my native country, yet I, seeing every sort and kind of people in their vocation and degree busily occupied about the commonwealth's affairs, and especially learned men daily putting forth in writing new inventions and devices to the furtherance of the same, thought it my bounden duty to God and to my country so to tumble my tub, I mean so to occupy and exercise myself in bestowing such spare hours as I, being at the beck and commandment of others, could conveniently win to myself, that though no commodity of that my labour and travail to the public weal should arise, yet it might by this appear that mine endeavour and goodwill hereunto was not lacking.

To the accomplishment, therefore, and fulfilling of this my mind and purpose, I took upon me to turn and translate out of Latin into our English tongue the fruitful and profitable book which Sir Thomas More, knight, compiled and made of the new isle Utopia, containing and setting forth the best state and form of a public weal, a work (as it appeareth) written almost forty years ago by the said Sir Thomas More the author thereof. The which man, forasmuch as he was a man of late time, yea almost of this our days, and for the excellent qualities wherewith the great goodness of God had plentifully endowed him, and for the high place and room whereunto his prince had most graciously called him, notably well known, not only among us his countrymen, but also in foreign countries and nations; therefore I have not much to speak of him. This only I say: that it is much to be lamented of all, and not only of us Englishmen, that a man of so incomparable wit, of so profound knowledge, of so absolute learning, and of so fine eloquence was yet nevertheless so much blinded, rather with obstinacy than with ignorance, that he could not or rather would not see the shining light of God's holy truth in certain principal points of Christian religion; but did rather choose to persevere

4

and continue in his wilful and stubborn obstinacy even to the very death. This I say is a thing much to be lamented. But letting this matter pass, I return again to *Utopia*. Which (as I said before) is a work not only for the matter that it containeth fruitful and profitable, but also for the writer's eloquent Latin style pleasant and delectable. Which he that readeth in Latin, as the author himself wrote it, perfectly understanding the same, doubtless he shall take great pleasure and delight both in the sweet eloquence of the writer and also in the witty invention and fine conveyance or disposition of the matter, but most of all in the good and wholesome lessons which be there in great plenty and abundance. But now I fear greatly that in this my simple translation, through my rudeness and ignorance in our English tongue, all the grace and pleasure of the eloquence wherewith the matter in Latin is finely set forth may seem to be utterly excluded and lost, and therefore the fruitfulness of the matter itself much peradventure diminished and appaired.

For who knoweth not, which knoweth anything, that an eloquent style setteth forth and highly commendeth a mean matter? Whereas on the other side rude and unlearned speech defaceth and disgraceth a very good matter. According as I heard once a wise man say, a good tale evil told were better untold, and an evil tale well told needeth none other solicitor. This thing I, well pondering and weighing with myself, and also knowing and acknowledging the barbarous rudeness of my translation, was fully determined never to have put it forth in print, had it not been for certain friends of mine, and especially one whom above all other I regarded, a man of sage and discreet wit and in worldly matters by long use well experienced, whose name is George Tadlowe, an honest citizen of London, and in the same city well accepted and of good reputation, at whose request and instance I first took upon my weak and feeble shoulders the heavy and weighty burden of this great enterprise. This man with divers other, but this man chiefly (for he was able to do more with me than many other), after that I had once rudely brought the work to an end, ceased not by all means possible continually to assault me until he had at the last, what by the force of his pithy arguments and strong reasons, and what by his authority so persuaded me, that he caused me to agree and consent to the imprinting hereof. He therefore, as the chief persuader, must take upon him the danger which upon this bold and rash enterprise shall ensue. I, as I suppose, am herein clearly acquit and discharged of all blame. Yet, honourable sir, for the better avoiding of envious and malicious tongues, I (knowing you to be a man not only profoundly learned and well affected towards all such as either can or will take pains in the well bestowing of that poor talent which God hath endued them with, but also for your godly disposition and virtuous qualities not unworthily now placed in authority and called to honour) am the bolder humbly to offer and dedicate unto your good mastership this my simple work. Partly that under the safe conduct of your protection it may the better be defended from the obloquy of them which can say well by nothing that pleaseth not their fond and corrupt judgments, though it be else both fruitful and godly, and partly that by the means of this homely present I may the better renew and revive (which of late, as you know, I have already begun to do) that old acquaintance that was between you and me in the time of our childhood, being then schoolfellows together. Not doubting that you for your native goodness and gentleness will accept in good part this poor gift, as an argument or token that mine old goodwill and hearty affection towards you is not, by reason of long tract of time and separation of our bodies, anything at all quailed and diminished, but rather (I assure you) much augmented and increased. This verily is the chief cause that hath encouraged me to be so bold with your mastership, else truly this my poor present is of such simple and mean sort, that it is neither able to recompense the least portion of your great gentleness to me, of my part undeserved, both in the time of our old acquaintance and also now lately again bountifully shewed, neither yet fit and meet for the very baseness of it to be offered to one so worthy as you be. But Almighty God (who therefore ever be thanked) hath advanced you to such fortune and dignity, that you be of ability to accept thankfully as well a man's goodwill as his gift. The same God grant you and all yours long and joyfully to continue in all godliness and prosperity.

THOMAS MORE TO PETER GILES,

SENDETH GREETING

I AM almost ashamed, right well beloved Peter Giles, to send unto you this book of the Utopian commonwealth wellnigh after a year's space, which I am sure you looked for within a month and a half. And no marvel, for you knew well enough that I was already disburdened of all the labour and study belonging to the invention in this work, and that I had no need at all to trouble my brains about the disposition or conveyance of the matter, and therefore had herein nothing else to do, but only to rehearse those things which you and I together heard master Raphael tell and declare. Wherefore there was no cause why I should study to set forth the matter with eloquence, forasmuch as his talk could not be fine and eloquent, being first not studied for, but sudden and unpremeditate, and then, as you know, of a man better seen in the Greek language than in the Latin tongue. And my writing, the nigher it should approach to his homely, plain, and simple speech, so much the nigher should it go to the truth, which is the only mark whereunto I do and ought to direct all my travail and study herein. I grant and confess, friend Peter, myself discharged of so much labour, having all these things ready done to my hand, that almost there was nothing left for me to do. Else either the invention or the disposition of this matter might have required of a wit neither base neither at all unlearned, both some time and leisure, and also some study. But if it were requisite and necessary that the matter should also have been written eloquently and not alone truly, of a surety that thing could I have performed by no time nor study. But now seeing all these cares, stays, and lets were taken away, wherein else so much labour and study should have been employed, and that there remained no other thing for me to do but only to write plainly the matter as I heard it spoken, that indeed was a thing light and easy to be done.

Howbeit, to the dispatching of this so little business, my other cares and troubles did leave almost less than no leisure. Whiles I do daily bestow my time about law matters, some to plead, some to hear, some as an arbitrator with mine award to determine, some as an umpire or a judge, with my sentence finally to discuss; whiles I go one way to see and visit my friend, another way about mine own private affairs; whiles I spend almost all the day abroad among others, and the residue at home among mine own; I leave to myself, I mean to my book, no time. For when I am come home I must commune with my wife, chat with my children, and talk with my servants. All the which things I reckon and account among business forasmuch as they must of necessity be done, and done must they needs be, unless a man will be stranger in his own house. And in any wise a man must so fashion and order his conditions and so appoint and dispose himself that he be merry, jocund, and pleasant among them whom either nature hath provided or chance hath made or he himself hath chosen to be the fellows and companions of his life, so that with too much gentle behaviour and familiarity he do not mar them, and by too much sufferance of his servants make them his masters. Among these things now rehearsed stealeth away the day, the month, the year. When do I write then? And all this while have I spoken no word of sleep, neither yet of meat, which among a great number doth waste no less time than doth sleep, wherein almost half the lifetime of man creepeth away. I therefore do win and get only that time which I steal from sleep and meat. Which time, because it is very little, and yet somewhat it is, therefore have I once at the last, though it be long first, finished *Utopia*, and have sent it to you, friend Peter, to read and peruse, to the intent that if anything have escaped me you might put me in remembrance of it.

For though in this behalf I do not greatly mistrust myself (which would God I were somewhat in wit and learning, as I am not all of the worst and dullest memory), yet have I not so great trust and confidence in it that I think nothing could fall out of my mind. For John Clement, my boy, who, as you know, was there present with us, whom I suffer to be away from no talk wherein may be any profit or goodness (for out of this young-bladed and new-shot-up corn, which hath already begun to spring up both in Latin and Greek learning, I look for plentiful increase at length of goodly ripe grain), he, I say, hath brought me into a great doubt. For whereas Hythloday (unless my memory fail me) said that the bridge of Amaurote which goeth over the river of Anyder is five hundred paces, that is to say half a mile, in length, my John saith that two hundred of those paces must be plucked away, for that the river containeth there not above three hundred paces in breadth; I pray you heartily call the matter to your remembrance. For if you agree with him I also will say as you say and confess myself deceived. But if you cannot remember the thing, then surely I will write as I have done and as mine own remembrance serveth me. For as I will take good heed that there be in my book nothing false, so if there be anything doubtful I will rather tell a lie than make a lie, because I had rather be good than wily. Howbeit, this matter may easily be remedied if you will take the pains to ask the question of Raphael himself by word of mouth, if he be now with you, or else by your letters. Which you must needs do for another doubt also that hath chanced, through whose fault I cannot tell, whether through mine or yours or Raphael's. For neither we remembered to inquire of him, nor he to tell us, in what part of the new world Utopia is situate. The which thing I had rather have spent no small sum of money than that it should thus have escaped us, as well for that I am ashamed to be ignorant in what sea that island standeth whereof I wrote so long a treatise, as also because there be with us certain men, and especially one virtuous and godly man and a professor of divinity, who is exceeding desirous to go unto Utopia, not for a vain and curious desire to see news, but to the intent he may further and increase our religion which is there already luckily begun. And that he may the better accomplish and perform this his good intent he is minded to procure that he may be sent thither by the high bishop; yea, and that he himself may be made bishop of Utopia, being nothing scrupulous herein that he must obtain this bishopric with suit. For he counteth that a godly suit which proceedeth not of the desire of honour or lucre, but only of a godly zeal. Wherefore I most earnestly desire you, friend Peter, to talk with Hythloday, if you can, face to face, or else to write your letters to him, and so to work in this matter that in this my book there may neither anything be found which is untrue, neither anything be lacking which is true. And I think verily it shall be well done that you shew unto him the book itself. For if I have missed or failed in any point, or if any fault have escaped me, no man can so well correct and amend it as he can; and yet that can he not do unless he peruse and read over my book written. Moreover, by this means shall you perceive whether he be well willing and content that I should undertake to put this work in writing. For if he be minded to publish and put forth his own labours and travels himself, perchance he would be loath, and so would I also, that in publishing the Utopian weal-public I should prevent him and take from him the flower and grace of the novelty of this his history. Howbeit, to say the very truth, I am not yet fully determined with myself whether I will put forth my book or no. For the natures of men be so diverse, the phantasies of some so wayward, their minds so unkind, their judgments so corrupt, that they which lead a merry and a jocund life, following their own sensual pleasures and carnal lusts, may seem to be in a much better state or case than they that vex and unquiet themselves with cares and study for the putting forth and publishing of something that may be either profit or pleasure to others, which others nevertheless will disdainfully, scornfully, and unkindly accept the same. The most part of all be unlearned, and a great number hath learning in contempt. The rude and barbarous alloweth nothing but that which is very barbarous indeed. If it be one that hath a little smack of learning, he rejecteth as homely gear and common ware whatsoever is not stuffed full of old moth-eaten terms and that be worn out of use. Some there be that have pleasure only in old rusty antiquities, and some only in their own doings. One is so sour, so crabbed, and so unpleasant, that he can away with no mirth nor sport. Another is so narrow between the shoulders, that he can bear no jests nor taunts. Some silly poor souls be so afeard that at every snappish word their nose shall be bitten off, that they stand in no less dread of every quick and sharp word than he that is bitten of a mad dog feareth water. Some be so mutable and wavering, that every hour they be in a new mind, saying one thing sitting and another thing standing. Another sort sitteth upon their ale-benches, and there among their cups they give judgment of the wits of writers, and with great authority they condemn, even as pleaseth them, every writer according to his writing, in most spiteful manner mocking, louting, and flouting them, being themselves in the mean season safe and, as saith the proverb, out of all danger of gunshot. For why, they be so smug and smooth, that they have not so much as one hair of an honest man whereby one may take hold of them. There be, moreover, some so unkind and ungentle, that, though they take great pleasure and delectation in the work, yet for all that they cannot find in their hearts to love the author thereof nor to afford him a good word, being much like uncourteous, unthankful, and churlish guests, which when they have with good and dainty meat well filled their bellies, depart home, giving no thanks to the feast maker. Go your ways now, and make a costly feast at your own charges for guests so dainty mouthed, so divers in taste, and besides that of so unkind and unthankful natures. But nevertheless, friend Peter, do, I pray you, with Hythloday as I willed you before. And as for this matter I shall be at my liberty afterwards to take new advisement. Howbeit, seeing I have taken great pains and labour in writing the matter, if it may stand with his mind and pleasure I will, as touching the edition of publishing of the book, follow the counsel and advice of my friends and specially yours. Thus fare you well, right heartily beloved friend Peter, with your gentle wife, and love me as you have ever done, for I love you better than ever I did.

THE FIRST BOOK OF UTOPIA

THE COMMUNICATION OF
RAPHAEL HYTHLODAY,

Concerning the best state
of a commonwealth

THE most victorious and triumphant king of England, Henry the eighth of that name, in all royal virtues a prince most peerless, had of late in controversy with Charles, the right high and mighty king of Castile, weighty matters and of great importance; for the debatement and final determination whereof the king's majesty sent me ambassador into Flanders, joined in commission with Cuthbert Tunstall, a man doubtless out of comparison and whom the king's majesty of late, to the great rejoicing of all men, did prefer to the office of Master of the Rolls.

But of this man's praises I will say nothing, not because I do fear that small credence shall be given to the testimony that cometh out of a friend's mouth; but because his virtue and learning be greater and of more excellence than that I am able to praise them, and also in all places so famous and so perfectly well known that they need not, nor ought not, of me to be praised, unless I would seem to shew and set forth the brightness of the sun with a candle, as the proverb saith.

There met us at Bruges (for thus it was before agreed) they whom their prince had for that matter appointed commissioners, excellent men all. The chief and the head of them was the Margrave (as they call him) of Bruges, a right honourable man: but the wisest and the best spoken of them was George Temsice, Provost of Cassel, a man not only by learning but also by nature of singular eloquence, and in the laws profoundly learned; but in reasoning and debating of matters, what by his natural wit and what by daily exercise, surely he had few fellows. After that we had once or twice met, and upon certain points or articles could not fully and thoroughly agree, they for a certain space took their leave of us and departed to Brussels, there to know their prince's pleasure.

I, in the meantime (for so my business lay), went straight thence to Antwerp. While I was there abiding, oftentimes among other but which to me was more welcome than any other, did visit me one Peter Giles, a citizen of Antwerp; a man there in his country of honest reputation, and also preferred to high promotions, worthy truly of the highest, for it is hard to say whether the young man be in learning or in honesty more excellent. For he is both of wonderful virtuous conditions, and also singularly well learned, and towards all sorts of people exceeding gentle; but towards his friends so kind-hearted, so loving, so faithful, so trusty, and of so earnest affection, that it were very hard in any place to find a man that with him in all points of friendship may be compared. No man can be more lowly or courteous. No man useth less simulation or dissimulation; in no man is more prudent simplicity. Besides this, he is in his talk and communication so merry and pleasant, yea and that without harm, that, through his gentle entertainment and his sweet and delectable communication, in me was greatly abated and diminished the fervent desire that I had to see my native country, my wife, and my children, whom then I did much long and covet to see, because that at that time I had been more than four months from them.

Upon a certain day when I had heard the divine service in our Lady's Church – which is the fairest, the most gorgeous, and curious church of building in all the city, and also most frequented of people – and, the service being done, was ready to go home to my lodging, I chanced to espy this foresaid Peter talking with a certain stranger, a man well stricken in age, with a black sun-burned face, a long beard, and a cloak cast homely about his shoulders, whom by his favour and apparel forthwith I judged to be a mariner. But the said Peter, seeing me, came unto me and saluted me. And as I was about to answer him: See you this man? saith he (and therewith he pointed to the man that I saw him talking with before). I was minded, quoth he, to bring him straight home to you.

He should have been very welcome to me, said I, for your sake.

Nay, quoth he, for his own sake, if you knew him; for there is no man this day living that can tell you of so many strange and unknown peoples and countries as this man can. And I know well that you be very desirous to hear of such news.

Then I conjectured not far amiss, quoth I, for even at the first sight I judged him to be a mariner.

Nay, quoth he, there ye were greatly deceived. He hath sailed indeed, not as the mariner Palinurus, but as the expert and prudent prince Ulysses; yea, rather as the ancient and sage philosopher Plato. For this same Raphael Hythloday (for this is his name) is very well learned in the Latin tongue, but profound and excellent in the Greek language, wherein he ever bestowed more study than in the Latin, because he had given himself wholly to the study of philosophy; whereof he knew that there is nothing extant in Latin that is to any purpose, saving a few of Seneca's and Cicero's doings. His patrimony that he was born unto he left to his brethren (for he is a Portuguese born), and for the desire that he had to see and know the far countries of the world, he joined himself in company with Amerigo Vespucci, and in the three last voyages of those four that be now in print and abroad in every man's hands, he continued still in his company, saving that in the last voyage he came not home again with him. For he made such means and shift, what by entreatance, and what by importune suit, that he got licence of Master Amerigo (though it were sore against his will) to be one of the twenty-three which in the end of the last voyage were left in the country of Gulike. He was therefore left behind for his mind sake, as one that took more thought and care for travelling than dying, having customarily in his mouth these sayings: He that hath no grave is covered with the sky, and, The way to heaven out of all places is of like length and distance. Which fantasy of his (if God had not been his better friend) he had surely bought full dear. But after the departing of Master Vespucci, when he had travelled through and about many countries with five of his companions Gulikians, at the last by marvellous chance he arrived in Taprobane, from whence he went to Calicut, where he chanced to find certain of his country ships, wherein he returned again into his country, nothing less than looked for.

All this when Peter had told me, I thanked him for his gentle kindness that he had vouchsafed to bring me to the speech of that man whose communication he thought should be to me pleasant and acceptable. And therewith I turned me to Raphael; and when we had hailed each other and had spoken those common words that be customarily spoken at the first meeting and acquaintance of strangers, we went thence to my house, and there in my garden, upon a bench covered with green turves, we sat down talking together. There he told us how that, after the departing of Vespucci, he and his fellows that tarried behind in Gulike began by little and little, through fair and gentle speech, to win the love and favour of the people of that country, insomuch that within short space they did dwell amongst them not only harmless, but also occupying with them very familiarly. He told us also that they were in high reputation and favour with a certain great man (whose name and country is now quite out of my remembrance) which of his mere liberality did bear the costs and charges of him and his five companions; and besides that gave them a trusty guide to conduct them in their journey (which by water was in boats and by land in wagons) and to bring them to other princes with very friendly commendations.

Thus after many days' journeys, he said, they found towns and cities and weal-publics, full of people, governed by good and wholesome laws. For under the line equinoctial, and on both sides of the same as far as the sun doth extend his course, lieth, quoth he, great and wide deserts and wildernesses, parched, burned, and dried up with continual and intolerable heat. All things be hideous, terrible, loathsome, and unpleasant to behold; all things out of fashion and comeliness, inhabited with wild beasts and serpents, or at the least wise with people that be no less savage, wild, and noisome than the very beasts themselves be. But a little farther beyond that, all things begin by little and little to wax pleasant; the air soft, temperate, and gentle; the ground covered with green grass; less wildness in the beasts. At the last shall ye come again to people, cities, and towns wherein is continual intercourse and occupying of merchandise and chaffare, not only among themselves and with their borderers, but also with merchants of far countries, both by land and water. There I had occasion, said he, to go to many countries on every side. For there was no ship ready to any voyage or journey, but I and my fellows were into it very gladly received. The ships that they found first were made plain, flat, and broad in the bottom, troughwise. The sails were made of great rushes, or of wickers, and in some places of leather. Afterwards they found ships with ridged keels and sails of canvas, yea, and shortly after, having all things like ours.

The shipmen also very expert and cunning, both in the sea and in the weather. But he said that he found great favour and friendship among them for teaching them the feat and the use of the lodestone, which to them before that time was unknown, and therefore they were wont to be very timorous and fearful upon the sea, nor to venture upon it, but only in the summer time. But now they have such a confidence in that stone, that they fear not stormy winter: in so doing farther from care than danger. Insomuch that it is greatly to be doubted lest that thing, through their own foolish hardiness, shall turn them to evil and harm, which at the first was supposed should be to them good and commodious.

But what he told us that he saw in every country where he came, it were very long to declare. Neither it is my purpose at this time to make rehearsal thereof. But peradventure in another place I will speak of it, chiefly such things as shall be profitable to be known, as in special be those decrees and ordinances that he marked to be well and wisely provided and enacted among such peoples as do live together in a civil policy and good order. For of such things did we busily inquire and demand of him, and he likewise very willingly told us of the same. But as for monsters, because they be no news, of them we were nothing inquisitive. For nothing is more easy to be found than be barking Scyllas, ravening Celænos, and Læstrygons, devourers of people, and suchlike great and incredible monsters. But to find citizens ruled by good and wholesome laws, that is an exceeding rare and hard thing. But as he marked many fond and foolish laws in those new found lands, so he rehearsed divers acts and constitutions whereby these our cities, nations, countries, and kingdoms may take example to amend their faults, enormities, and errors. Whereof in another place (as I said) I will entreat.

Now at this time I am determined to rehearse only that he told us of the manners, customs, laws, and ordinances of the Utopians. But first I will repeat our former communication by the occasion and (as I might say) the drift whereof he was brought into the mention of that wealpublic. For, when Raphael had very prudently touched divers things that be amiss, some here and some there, yea, very many on both parts; and again had spoken of such wise laws and prudent decrees as be established and used, both here among us and also there among them, as a man so perfect and expert in the laws and customs of every several country, as though into what place soever he came guestwise there he had led all his life: then Peter, much marvelling at the man: Surely, Master Raphael, quoth he, I wonder greatly why you get you not into some king's court. For I am sure there is no prince living, that would not be very glad of you, as a man not only able highly to delight him with your profound learning and this your knowledge of countries and peoples, but also meet to instruct him with examples and help him with counsel. And thus doing, you shall bring yourself in a very good case, and also be of ability to help all your friends and kinsfolk.

As concerning my friends and kinsfolk, quoth he, I pass not greatly for them. For I think I have sufficiently done my part towards them already. For these things that other men do not depart from until they be old and sick, yea, which they be then very loath to leave when they can no longer keep, those very same things did I, being not only lusty and in good health, but also in the flower of my youth, divide among my friends and kinsfolk. Which I think with this my liberality ought to hold them contented, and not to require nor to look that besides this I should for their sakes give myself in bondage unto kings.

Nay, God forbid that, quoth Peter, it is not my mind that you should be in bondage to kings, but as a retainer to them at your pleasure. Which surely I think is the nighest way that you can devise how to bestow your time fruitfully, not only for the private commodity of your friends and for the general profit of all sorts of people, but also for the advancement of yourself to a much wealthier state and condition than you be now in.

To a wealthier condition, quoth Raphael, by that means that my mind standeth clean against? Now I live at liberty after mine own mind and pleasure, which I think very few of these great states and peers of realms can say. Yea, and there be enough of them that sue for great men's friendships, and therefore think it no great hurt if they have not me, nor three or four such other as I am.

Well, I perceive plainly, friend Raphael, quoth I, that you be desirous neither of riches nor of power; and truly I have in no less reverence and estimation a man of your mind than any of them all that be so high in power and authority. But you shall do as it becometh you: yea, and according to this wisdom, to this high and free courage of yours, if you can find in your heart so to appoint and dispose yourself that you may apply your wit and diligence to the profit of the weal-public, though it be somewhat to your own pain and hindrance. And this shall you never so well do, nor with so great profit perform, as if you be of some great prince's council, and put into his head (as I doubt not but you will) honest opinions and virtuous persuasions. For from the prince, as from a perpetual well-spring, cometh among the people the flood of all that is good or evil. But in you is so perfect learning that, without any experience, and again so great experience that without any learning you may well be any king's counsellor.

You be twice deceived, Master More, quoth he, first in me and again in the thing itself. For neither is in me the ability that you force upon me, and if it were never so much, yet in disquieting mine own quietness I should nothing further the weal-public. For, first of all, the most part of all princes have more delight in warlike matters and feats of chivalry (the knowledge whereof I neither have nor desire) than in the good feats of peace, and employ much more study how by right or by wrong to enlarge their dominions, than how well and peaceable to rule and govern that they have already. Moreover, they that be counsellors to kings, every one of them either is of himself so wise indeed that he needeth not, or else he thinketh himself so wise that he will not, allow another man's counsel, saving that they do shamefully and flatteringly give assent to the fond and foolish sayings of certain great men, whose favours, because they be in high authority with their prince, by assentation and flattery they labour to obtain. And verily it is naturally given to all men to esteem their own inventions best. So both the raven and the ape think their own young ones fairest. Then if a man in such a company, where some disdain and have despite at other men's inventions and some count their own best, if among such men (I say) a man should bring forth anything that he hath read done in times past or that he hath seen done in other places, there the hearers fare as though the whole existimation of their wisdom were in jeopardy to be overthrown, and that ever after they should be counted for very dizzards, unless they could in other men's inventions pick out matter to reprehend and find fault at. If all other poor helps fail, then this is their extreme refuge. These things, say they, pleased our forefathers and ancestors; would God we could be so wise as they were. And, as though they had wittily concluded the matter, and with this answer stopped every man's mouth, they sit down again. As who should say it were a very dangerous matter if a man in any point should be found wiser than his forefathers were. And yet be we content to suffer the best and wittiest of their decrees to lie unexecuted: but if in anything a better order might have been taken than by them was, there we take fast hold, finding therein many faults. Many times have I chanced upon such proud, lewd, overthwart, and wayward judgments, yea, and once in England.

I pray you, sir, quoth I, have you been in our country?

Yea forsooth, quoth he, and there I tarried for the space of four or five months together, not long after the insurrection that the western Englishmen made against their king, which by their own miserable and pitiful slaughter was suppressed and ended. In the mean season I was much bound and beholden to the right reverend father, John Morton, Archbishop and Cardinal of Canterbury, and at that time also Lord Chancellor of England: a man, Master Peter (for Master More knoweth already that I will say), not more honourable for his authority than for his prudence and virtue. He was of a mean stature, and though stricken in age, yet bare he his body upright. In his face did shine such an amiable reverence as was pleasant to behold; gentle in communication, yet earnest, and sage. He had great delight many times with rough speech to his suitors, to prove, but without harm, what prompt wit and what bold spirit were in every man. In the which, as in a virtue much agreeing with his nature so that therewith were not joined impudency, he took great delectation. And the same person, as apt and meet to have an administration in the weal-public, he did lovingly embrace. In his speech he was fine, eloquent, and pithy. In the law he had profound knowledge, in wit he was incomparable, and in memory wonderful excellent. These qualities, which in him were by nature singular, he by learning and use had made perfect. The king put much trust in his counsel, the weal-public also, in a manner, leaned unto him when I was there. For even in the chief of his youth he was taken from school into the court, and there passed all his time in much trouble and business, being continually tumbled and tossed in the waves of divers misfortunes and adversities. And so by many and great dangers he learned the experience of the world, which so being learned cannot easily be forgotten.

It chanced on a certain day, when I sat at his table, there was also a certain layman cunning in the laws of your realm. Who, I cannot tell whereof taking occasion, began diligently and earnestly to praise that strait and rigorous justice which at that time was there executed upon felons, who, as he said, were for the most part twenty hanged together upon one gallows. And, seeing so few escaped punishment, he said he could not choose but greatly wonder and marvel, how and by what evil luck it should so come to pass that thieves, nevertheless, were in every place so rife and so rank.

Nay, sir, quoth I (for I durst boldly speak my mind before the cardinal), marvel nothing hereat: for this punishment of thieves passeth the limits of justice, and is also very hurtful to the weal-public. For it is too extreme and cruel a punishment for theft, and yet not sufficient to refrain and withhold men from theft. For simple theft is not so great an offence that it ought to be punished with death. Neither there is any punishment so horrible that it can keep them from stealing which have no other craft whereby to get their living. Therefore in this point not you only but also the most part of the world be like evil schoolmasters, which be readier to beat than to teach their scholars. For great and horrible punishments be appointed for thieves, whereas much rather provision should have been made that there were some means whereby they might get their living, so that no man should be driven to this extreme necessity, first to steal and then to die.

Yes, quoth he, this matter is well enough provided for already. There be handicrafts, there is husbandry to get their living by, if they would not willingly be nought.

Nay, quoth I, you shall not escape so: for, first of all, I will speak nothing of them that come home out of the wars maimed and lame, as not long ago out of Blackheath field and a little before that out of the wars in France; such, I say, as put their lives in jeopardy for the weal-public's or the king's sake, and by reason of weakness and lameness be not able to occupy their old crafts, and be too aged to learn new: of them I will speak nothing, forasmuch as wars have their ordinary recourse. But let us consider those things that chance daily before our eyes.

First there is a great number of gentlemen which cannot be content to live idle themselves, like dors, of that which others have laboured for: their tenants, I mean, whom they poll and shave to the quick by raising their rents (for this only point of frugality do they use, men else, through their lavish and prodigal spending, able to bring themselves to very beggary); these gentlemen, I say, do not only live in idleness themselves, but also carry about with them at their tails a great flock or train of idle and loitering serving-men, which never learned any craft whereby to get their livings. These men, as soon as their master is dead, or be sick themselves, be incontinent thrust out of doors. For gentlemen had rather keep idle persons than sick men, and many times the dead man's heir is not able to maintain so great a house and keep so many serving-men as his father did. Then in the mean season they that be thus destitute of service either starve for hunger or manfully play the thieves. For what would you have them to do? When they have wandered abroad so long, until they have worn threadbare their apparel and also appaired their health, then gentlemen, because of their pale and sickly faces and patched coats, will not take them into service. And husbandmen dare not set them a-work; knowing well enough that he is nothing meet to do true and faithful service to a poor man with a spade and a mattock for small wages and hard fare, which, being daintily and tenderly pampered up in idleness and pleasure, was wont with a sword and a buckler by his side to jet through the street with a bragging look and to think himself too good to be any man's mate. Nay, by Saint Mary, sir, quoth the lawyer, not so. For this kind of men must we make most of. For in them, as men of stouter stomachs, bolder spirits, and manlier courages than handi-craftsmen and plowmen be, doth consist the whole power, strength, and puissance of our army, when we must fight in battle.

Forsooth, sir, as well you might say, quoth I, that for war's sake you must cherish thieves; for surely you shall never lack thieves while you have them. No, nor thieves be not the most false and faint-hearted soldiers, nor soldiers be not the cowardliest thieves: so well these two crafts agree together. But this fault, though it be much used among you, yet is it not peculiar to you only, but common also almost to all nations.

Yet France besides this is troubled and infected with a much sorer plague. The whole realm is filled and besieged with hired soldiers in peace time (if that be peace) which be brought in under the same colour and pretence that hath persuaded you to keep these idle serving-men. For these wise fools and very archdolts thought the wealth of the whole country herein to consist, if there were ever in a readiness a strong and sure garrison, specially of old practised soldiers, for they put no trust at all in men unexercised. And therefore they must be forced to seek for war, to the end they may ever have practised soldiers and cunning manslayers, lest that (as it is prettily said of Sallust) their hands and their minds, through idleness or lack of exercise, should wax dull. But how pernicious and pestilent a thing it is to maintain such beasts the Frenchmen by their own harms have learned, and the examples of the Romans, Carthaginians, Syrians, and of many other countries do manifestly declare. For not only the empire but also the fields and cities of all these by divers occasions have been overrunned and destroyed of their own armies beforehand had in a readiness. Now how unnecessary a thing this is hereby it may appear, that the French soldiers, which from their youth have been practised and inured in feats of arms, do not crack nor advance themselves to have very often got the upper hand and mastery of your new-made and unpractised soldiers. But in this point I will not use many words, lest perchance I may seem to flatter you. No, nor those same handicraftsmen of yours in cities, nor yet the rude and uplandish plowmen of the country, are not supposed to be greatly afraid of your gentlemen's idle serving-men, unless it be such as be not of body or stature correspondent to their strength and courage, or else whose bold stomachs be discouraged through poverty.

Thus you may see that it is not to be feared lest they should be effeminated if they were brought up in good crafts and laboursome works whereby to get their livings, whose stout and sturdy bodies (for gentlemen vouchsafe to corrupt and spill none but picked and chosen men) now, either by reason of rest and idleness be brought to weakness, or else by too easy and womanly exercises be made feeble and unable to endure hardness. Truly, howsoever the case standeth, this, methinketh, is nothing available to the weal-public, for war sake, which you never have but when you will yourselves, to keep and maintain an innumerable flock of that sort of men that be so troublesome and noyous in peace, whereof you ought to have a thousand times more regard, than of war. But yet this is not only the necessary cause of stealing. There is another, which, as I suppose, is proper and peculiar to you Englishmen alone.

What is that? quoth the cardinal.

Forsooth, my lord, quoth I, your sheep that were wont to be so meek and tame and so small eaters, now, as I hear say, be become so great devourers and so wild, that they eat up and swallow down the very men themselves. They consume, destroy, and devour whole fields, houses, and cities. For look in what parts of the realm doth grow the finest and therefore dearest wool, there noblemen and gentlemen, yea and certain abbots, holy men no doubt, not contenting themselves with the yearly revenues and profits that were wont to grow to their forefathers and predecessors of their lands, nor being content that they live in rest and pleasure nothing profiting, yea, much annoying the weal-public, leave no ground for tillage. They enclose all into pastures; they throw down houses; they pluck down towns, and leave nothing standing but only the church to be made a sheep-house. And as though you lost no small quantity of ground by forests, chases, lands, and parks, those good holy men turn all dwelling places and all glebeland into desolation and wilderness. Therefore that one covetous and insatiable cormorant and very plague of its native country may compass about and enclose many thousand acres of ground together within one pale or hedge, the husbandmen be thrust out of their own, or else either by covin and fraud or by violent oppression they be put besides it, or by wrongs and injuries they be so wearied, that they be compelled to sell all. By one means, therefore, or by other, either by hook or crook, they must needs depart away, poor, silly, wretched souls, men, women, husbands, wives, fatherless children, widows, woeful mothers with their young babes, and their whole household small in substance and much in number, as husbandry requireth many hands. Away they trudge, I say, out of their known and accustomed houses, finding no place to rest in. All their household stuff, which is very little worth though it might well abide the sale, yet being suddenly thrust out they be constrained to sell it for a thing of nought. And when they have wandered abroad till that be spent, what can they then else do but steal, and then justly pardy be hanged, or else go about a-begging? And yet then also they be cast in prison as vagabonds, because they go about and work not, whom no man will set a-work, though they never so willingly proffer themselves thereto.

For one shepherd or herdman is enough to eat up that ground with cattle, to the occupying whereof about husbandry many hands were requisite. And this is also the cause why victuals be now in many places dearer. Yea, besides this the price of wool is so risen, that poor folks, which were wont to work it and make cloth thereof, be now able to buy none at all. And by this means very many be forced to forsake work and to give themselves to idleness. For after that so much ground was enclosed for pasture an infinite multitude of sheep died of the rot, such vengeance God took of their inordinate and insatiable covetousness, sending among the sheep that pestiferous murrain which much more justly should have fallen on the sheepmasters' own heads. And though the number of sheep increase never so fast, yet the price falleth not one mite, because there be so few sellers; for they be almost all come into a few rich men's hands, whom no need forceth to sell before they lust, and they lust not before they may sell as dear as they lust.

Now the same cause bringeth in like dearth of the other kinds of cattle, yea, and that so much the more because that after farms plucked down and husbandry decayed there is no man that passeth for the breeding of young store. For these rich men bring not up the young ones of great cattle as they do lambs. But first they buy them abroad very cheap, and afterward, when they be fatted in their pastures, they sell them again exceeding dear. And therefore (as I suppose) the whole incommodity hereof is not yet felt; for yet they make dearth only in those places where they sell. But when they shall fetch them away from thence where they be bred faster than they can be brought up, then shall there also be felt great dearth, store beginning there to fail where the ware is bought. Thus the unreasonable covetousness of a few hath turned that thing to the utter undoing of your island, in the which thing the chief felicity of your realm did consist. For this great dearth of victuals causeth men to keep as little houses and as small hospitality as they possibly may, and to put away their servants; whither, I pray you, but a-begging, or else (which these gentle bloods and stout stomachs will sooner set their minds unto) a-stealing?

Now to amend the matter, to this wretched beggary and miserable poverty is joined great wantonness, importunate superfluity, and excessive riot. For not only gentlemen's servants, but also handicraftsmen, yea, and almost the plowmen of the country, with all other sorts of people, use much strange and proud newfangleness in their apparel, and too much prodigal riot and sumptuous fare at their table. Now bawds, queans, whores, harlots, strumpets, brothel-houses, stews; and yet another stews, wine-taverns, ale-houses, and tippling houses, with so many naughty, lewd, and unlawful games, as dice, cards, tables, tennis, bowls, quoits, do not all these send the haunters of them straight a-stealing, when their money is gone? Cast out these pernicious abominations; make a law that they which plucked down farms and towns of husbandry shall re-edify them, or else yield and uprender the possession thereof to such as will go to the cost of building them anew. Suffer not these rich men to buy up all to engross and forestall, and with their monopoly to keep the market alone as please them. Let not so many be brought up in idleness; let husbandry and tillage be restored; let clothworking be renewed, that there may be honest labours for this idle sort to pass their time in profitably, which hitherto either poverty hath caused to be thieves, or else now be either vagabonds or idle serving men, and shortly will be thieves.

Doubtless unless you find a remedy for these enormities you shall in vain advance yourselves of executing justice upon felons. For this justice is more beautiful in appearance and more flourishing to the shew than either just or profitable. For by suffering your youth wantonly and viciously to be brought up, and to be infected, even from their tender age, by little and little with vice, then, a God's name, to be punished when they commit the same faults after being come to man's state, which from their youth they were ever like to do; in this point, I pray you, what other thing do you than make thieves and then punish them?

Now as I was thus speaking, the lawyer began to make himself ready to answer, and was determined with himself to use the common fashion and trade of disputers, which be more diligent in rehearsing than answering, as thinking the memory worthy of the chief praise. Indeed, sir, quoth he, you have said well, being but a stranger and one that might rather hear something of these matters, than have any exact or perfect knowledge of the same, as I will incontinent by open proof make manifest and plain. For first I will rehearse in order all that you have said; then I will declare wherein you be deceived through lack of knowledge in all our fashions, manners, and customs; and last of all I will answer your arguments, and confute them every one. First therefore I will begin where I promised. Four things you seemed to me—

Hold your peace, quoth the cardinal, for it appeareth that you will make no short answer, which make such a beginning. Wherefore at this time you shall not take the pains to make your answer, but keep it to your next meeting, which I would be right glad that it might be even to-morrow next, unless either you or master Raphael have any earnest let. But now, Master Raphael, I would very gladly hear of you, why you think theft not worthy to be punished with death, or what other punishment you can devise more expedient to the weal-public. For I am sure you are not of that mind, that you would have theft escape unpunished. For if now the extreme punishment of death cannot cause them to leave stealing, then, if ruffians and robbers should be sure of their lives, what violence, what fear, were able to hold their hands from robbing which would take the mitigation of the punishment as a very provocation to the mischief?

Surely, my lord, quoth I, I think it not right nor justice that the loss of money should cause the loss of man's life. For mine opinion is, that all the goods in the world are not able to countervail man's life. But if they would thus say, that the breaking of justice and the transgression of the laws is recompensed with this punishment, and not the loss of the money, then why may not this extreme and rigorous justice well be called plain injury? For so cruel governance, so strict rules and unmerciful laws be not allowable, that if a small offence be committed, by and by the sword should be drawn. Nor so stoical ordinances are to be borne withal, as to count all offences of such equality, that the killing of a man or the taking of his money from him were both a matter, and the one no more heinous offence than the other, between the which two, if we have any respect to equity, no similitude or equality consisteth. God commandeth us that we shall not kill. And be we then so hasty to kill a man for taking a little money? And if any man would understand killing by this commandment of God to be forbidden after no larger wise than man's constitutions define killing to be lawful, then why may it not likewise by man's constitutions be determined after what sort whoredom, fornication, and perjury may be lawful? For whereas, by the permission of God, no man hath power to kill neither himself nor yet any other man, then, if a law made by the consent of men concerning slaughter of men ought to be of such strength, force, and virtue, that they which contrary to the commandment of God have killed those whom this constitution of man commanded to be killed, be clean quit and exempt out of the bonds and danger of God's commandment, shall it not then, by this reason follow that the power of God's commandment shall extend no further than man's law doth define and permit? And so shall it come to pass, that in like manner man's constitutions in all things shall determine how far the observation of all God's commandments shall extend. To be short, Moses' law, though it were ungentle and sharp, as a law that was given to bondmen, yea, and them very obstinate, stubborn, and stiff-necked, yet it punished theft by the purse, and not with death. And let us not think that God in the new law of clemency and mercy, under the which He ruleth us with fatherly gentleness, as His dear children, hath given us greater scope and licence to the execution of cruelty one upon another.

Now ye have heard the reasons whereby I am persuaded that this punishment is unlawful. Furthermore, I think there is nobody that knoweth not how unreasonable, yea, how pernicious a thing it is to the weal-public that a thief and an homicide or murderer should suffer equal and like punishment. For the thief, seeing that man that is condemned for theft in no less jeopardy nor judged to no less punishment than him that is convict of manslaughter, through this cogitation only he is strongly and forcibly provoked, and in a manner constrained, to kill him whom else he would have but robbed. For the murder being once done, he is in less fear and in more hope that the deed shall not be betrayed or known, seeing the party is now dead and rid out of the way, which only might have uttered and disclosed it. But if he chance to be taken and descried, yet he is in no more danger and jeopardy than if he had committed but single felony. Therefore while we go about with such cruelty to make thieves afraid, we provoke them to kill good men.

Now as touching this question, what punishment were more commodious and better, that truly in my judgment is easier to be found than what punishment might be worse. For why should we doubt that to be a good and a profitable way for the punishment of offenders, which we know did in times past so long please the Romans, men in the administration of a weal-public most expert, politic, and cunning? Such as among them were convict of great and heinous trespasses, them they condemned into stone quarries, and into mines to dig metal, there to be kept in chains all the days of their life. But as concerning this matter, I allow the ordinance of no nation so well as that which I saw, while I travelled abroad about the world, used in Persia among the people that commonly be called the Polylerites, whose land is both large and ample and also well and wittily governed, and the people in all conditions free and ruled by their own laws, saving that they pay a yearly tribute to the great king of Persia. But because they be far from the sea, compassed and enclosed almost round about with high mountains, and do content themselves with the fruits of their own land, which is of itself very fertile and fruitful, for this cause neither they go to other countries, nor other come to them. And according to the old custom of the land they desire not to enlarge the bounds of their dominions; and those that they have by reason of the high hills be easily defended, and the tribute which they pay to their chief lord and king setteth them quit and free from warfare. Thus their life is commodious rather than gallant, and may better be called happy or wealthy than notable or famous. For they be not known as much as by name, I suppose, saving only to their next neighbours and borderers.

They that in this land be attainted and convict of felony, make restitution of that which they stole to the right owner, and not (as they do in other lands) to the king, whom they think to have no more right to the thief-stolen thing than the thief himself hath. But if the thing be lost or made away, then the value of it is paid of the goods of such offenders, which else remaineth all whole to their wives and children. And they themselves be condemned to be common labourers; and, unless the theft be very heinous, they be neither locked in prison nor fettered in gyves, but be untied and go at large, labouring in the common works. They that refuse labour, or go slowly and slackly to their work, be not only tied in chains, but also pricked forward with stripes; but being diligent about their work they live without check or rebuke. Every night they be called in by name, and be locked in their chambers. Beside their daily labour, their life is nothing hard or incommodious. Their fare is indifferent good, borne at the charges of the weal-public, because they be common servants to the commonwealth. But their charges in all places of the land are not borne alike, for in some parts that which is bestowed upon them is gathered of alms. And though that way be uncertain, yet the people be so full of mercy and pity, that none is found more profitable or plentiful. In some places certain lands be appointed hereunto, of the revenues whereof they be maintained; and in some places every man giveth a certain tribute for the same use and purpose.

Again, in some parts of the land these serving-men (for so be these damned persons called) do no common work, but as every private man needeth labourers, so he cometh into the market-place and there hireth some of them for meat and drink and a certain limited wages by the day, somewhat cheaper than he should hire a free man. It is also lawful for them to chastise the sloth of these serving-men with stripes. By this means they never lack work, and besides the gaining of their meat and drink, every one of them bringeth daily something into the common treasury. All and every one of them be apparelled in one colour. Their heads be not polled or shaven, but rounded a little above the ears, and the tip of the one ear is cut off. Every one of them may take meat and drink of their friends, and also a coat of their own colour; but to receive money is death, as well to the giver as to the receiver. And no less jeopardy it is for a free man to receive money of a serving-man for any manner of cause, and likewise for serving-men to touch weapons. The serving-men of every several shire be distinct and known from other by their several and distinct badges which to cast away is death, as it is also to be seen out of the precinct of their own shire, or to talk with a serving-man of another shire.

And it is no less danger to them for to intend to run away than to do it indeed. Yea, and to conceal such an enterprise in a serving-man it is death, in a free man servitude. Of the contrary part, to him that openeth and uttereth such counsels be decreed large gifts, to a free man a great sum of money, to a serving-man freedom, and, to them both, forgiveness and pardon of that they were of counsel in that pretence. So that it can never be so good for them to go forward in their evil purpose as, by repentance, to turn back.

This is the law and order in this behalf, as I have shewed you. Wherein what humanity is used, how far it is from cruelty, and how commodious it is, you do plainly perceive, forasmuch as the end of their wrath and punishment intendeth nothing else but the destruction of vices and saving of men, with so using and ordering them that they cannot choose but be good, and what harm soever they did before, in the residue of their life to make amends for the same. Moreover it is so little feared that they should turn again to their vicious conditions, that wayfaring men will for their safeguard choose them to their guides before any other, in every shire changing and taking new; for if they would commit robbery they have nothing about them meet for that purpose. They may touch no weapons; money found about them should betray the robbery. They should be no sooner taken with the manner, but forthwith they should be punished. Neither they can have any hope at all to scape away by fleeing. For how should a man that in no part of his apparel is like other men fly privily and unknown, unless he would run away naked? Howbeit, so also fleeing he should be descried by the rounding of his head and his ear mark. But it is a thing to be doubted that they will lay their heads together and conspire against the weal-public. No, no, I warrant you. For the serving-men of one shire alone could never hope to bring to pass such an enterprise without soliciting, enticing, and alluring the serving-men of many other shires to take their parts.

Which thing is to them so impossible, that they may not as much as speak or talk together or salute one another. No, it is not to be thought that they would make their own countrymen and companions of their counsel in such a matter, which they know well should be jeopardy to the concealer thereof and great commodity and goodness to the opener and detector of the same. Whereas, on the other part, there is none of them all hopeless or in despair to recover again his former state of freedom by humble obedience, by patient suffering, and by giving good tokens and likelihood of himself, that he will ever after that live like a true and an honest man. For every year divers of them be restored to their freedom through the commendation of their patience.

When I had thus spoken, saying moreover that I could see no cause why this order might not be had in England with much more profit than the justice which the lawyer so highly praised, Nay, quoth the lawyer, this could never be so stablished in England but that it must needs bring the weal-public into great jeopardy and hazard. And, as he was thus saying, he shaked his head and made a wry mouth, and so he held his peace. And all that were there present with one assent agreed to his saying.

Well, quoth the cardinal, yet it were hard to judge without a proof whether this order would do well here or no. But when the sentence of death is given, if then the king should command execution to be deferred and spared, and would prove this order and fashion, taking away the privileges of all sanctuaries, if then the proof should declare the thing to be good and profitable, then it were well done that it were stablished; else the con-demned and reprieved persons may as well and as justly be put to death after this proof as when they were first cast. Neither any jeopardy can in the mean space grow hereof. Yea, and methinketh that these vagabonds may very well be ordered after the same fashion, against whom we have hitherto made so many laws and so little prevailed.

When the cardinal had thus said, then every man gave great praise to my sayings, which a little before they had disallowed. But most of all was esteemed that which was spoken of vagabonds, because it was the cardinal's own addition. I cannot tell whether it were best to rehearse the communication that followed, for it was not very sad; but yet you shall hear it, for there was no evil in it, and partly it pertained to the matter before said.

There chanced to stand by a certain jesting parasite or scoffer, which would seem to resemble and counterfeit the fool. But he did in such wise counterfeit, that he was almost the very same indeed that he laboured to represent. He so studied with words and sayings brought forth so out of time and place to make sport and move laughter, that he himself was oftener laughed at than his jests were. Yet the foolish fellow brought out now and then such indifferent and reasonable stuff, that he made the proverb true, which saith: He that shooteth oft, at the last shall hit the mark. So that when one of the company said that through my communication a good order was found for thieves, and that the cardinal also had well provided for vagabonds, so that only remained some good provision to be made for them that through sickness and age were fallen into poverty and were become so impotent and unwieldy that they were not able to work for their living: Tush, quoth he, let me alone with them; you shall see me do well enough with them. For I had rather than any good that this kind of people were driven somewhere out of my sight, they have so sore troubled me many times and oft when they have with their lamentable tears begged money of me: and yet they could never to my mind so tune their song that thereby they ever got of me one farthing. For evermore the one of these two chanced: either that I would not, or else that I could not because I had it not. Therefore now they be waxed wise; for when they see me go by, because they will not lose their labour, they let me pass and say not one word to me. So they look for nothing of me, no, in good sooth, no more than if I were a priest or a monk. But I will make a law, that all these beggars shall be distributed and bestowed into houses of religion. The men shall be made lay brethren, as they call them, and the women nuns.

Hereat the cardinal smiled, and allowed it in jest, yea, and all the residue in good earnest. But a certain friar, graduate in divinity, took such pleasure and delight in this jest of priests and monks, that he also being else a man of grisly and stern gravity, began merrily and wantonly to jest and taunt. Nay, quoth he, you shall not so be rid and dispatched of beggars unless you make some provision also for us friars.

Why, quoth the jester, that is done already, for my lord himself set a very good order for you when he decreed that vagabonds should be kept strait, and set to work; for you be the greatest and veriest vagabonds that be.

This jest also, when they saw the cardinal not disprove it, every man took it gladly, saving only the friar. For he (and that no marvel) being thus touched on the quick, and hit on the gall, so fret, so fumed, and chafed at it, and was in such a rage, that he could not refrain himself from chiding, scolding, railing, and reviling. He called the fellow ribald, villain, javel, backbiter, slanderer, and the child of perdition, citing therewith terrible threatenings out of Holy Scripture.

Then the jesting scoffer began to play the scoffer indeed, and verily he was good at that, for he could play a part in that play, no man better. Patient yourself, good master friar, quoth he, and be not angry, for Scripture saith: In your patience you shall save your souls.

Then the friar (for I will rehearse his own very words): No, gallows wretch, I am not angry, quoth he, or at the least wise I do not sin; for the Psalmist saith, Be you angry, and sin not. Then the cardinal spake gently to the friar, and desired him to quiet himself.

No, my lord, quoth he, I speak not but of a good zeal as I ought, for holy men had a good zeal. Wherefore it is said: The zeal of thy house hath eaten me. And it is sung in the church. The scorners of Elisha, while he went up into the house of God, felt the zeal of the bald, as peradventure this scorning villain ribald shall feel.

You do it, quoth the cardinal, perchance of a good mind and affection; but methinketh you should do, I cannot tell whether more holily, certes more wisely, if you would not set your wit to a fool's wit, and with a fool take in hand a foolish contention.

No, forsooth, my lord, quoth he, I should not do more wisely. For Solomon the wise saith: Answer a fool according to his folly, like as I do now, and do shew him the pit that he shall fall into if he take not heed. For if many scorners of Elisha, which was but one bald man, felt the zeal of the bald, how much more shall one scorner of many friars feel, among whom be many bald men? And we have also the pope's bulls, whereby all that mock and scorn us be excommunicate, suspended, and accursed.

The cardinal, seeing that none end would be made, sent away the jester by a privy beck, and turned the communication to another matter. Shortly after, when he was risen from the table, he went to hear his suitors, and so dismissed us.

Look, Master More, with how long and tedious a tale I have kept you, which surely I would have been ashamed to have done, but that you so earnestly desired me, and did after such a sort give ear unto it as though you would not that any parcel of that communication should be left out. Which though I have done somewhat briefly, yet could I not choose but rehearse it for the judgment of them which, when they had disproved and disallowed my sayings, yet incontinent, hearing the cardinal allow them, did themselves also approve the same, so impudently flattering him, that they were nothing ashamed to admit, yea, almost in good earnest, his jester's foolish inventions, because that he himself by smiling at them did seem not to disprove them. So that hereby you may right well perceive how little the courtiers would regard and esteem me and my sayings.

I ensure you, Master Raphael, quoth I, I took great delectation in hearing you; all things that you said were spoken so wittily and so pleasantly. And methought myself to be in the meantime not only at home in my country, but also through the pleasant remembrance of the cardinal, in whose house I was brought up of a child, to wax a child again. And, friend Raphael, though I did bear very great love towards you before, yet seeing you do so earnestly favour this man, you will not believe how much my love towards you is now increased. But yet, all this notwithstanding, I can by no means change my mind, but that I must needs believe that you, if you be disposed and can find in your heart to follow some prince's court, shall with your good counsels greatly help and further the commonwealth. Wherefore there is nothing more appertaining to your duty, that is to say to the duty of a good man. For whereas your Plato judgeth that weal-publics shall by this means attain perfect felicity, either if philosophers be kings, or else if kings give themselves to the study of philosophy, how far, I pray you, shall commonwealths then be from this felicity, if philosophers will vouchsafe to instruct kings with their good counsel?

They be not so unkind, quoth he, but they would gladly do it, yea, many have done it already in books that they have put forth, if kings and princes would be willing and ready to follow good counsel. But Plato doubtless did well foresee, unless kings themselves would apply their minds to the study of philosophy, that else they would never thoroughly allow the counsel of philosophers, being themselves before, even from their tender age, infected and corrupt with perverse and evil opinions. Which thing Plato himself proved true in King Dionysius. If I should propose to any king wholesome decrees, doing my endeavour to pluck out of his mind the pernicious original causes of vice and naughtiness, think you not that I should forthwith either be driven away or else made a laughing-stock? Well, suppose I were with the French king, and there sitting in his council while in that most secret consultation, the king himself there being present in his own person, they beat their brains, and search the very bottoms of their wits to discuss by what craft and means the king may still keep Milan and draw to him again fugitive Naples; and then how to conquer the Venetians, and how to bring under his jurisdiction all Italy; then how to win the dominion of Flanders, Brabant, and of all Burgundy with divers other lands whose kingdoms he hath long ago in mind and purpose invaded. Here while one counselleth to conclude a league of peace with the Venetians, so long to endure as shall be thought meet and expedient for their purpose, and to make them also of their counsel, yea, and besides that to give them part of the prey which afterward, when they have brought their purpose about after their own minds, they may require and claim again, another thinketh best to hire the Germans. Another would have the favour of the Swiss won with money. Another's advice is to appease the puissant power of the emperor's majesty with gold as with a most pleasant and acceptable sacrifice. While another giveth counsel to make peace with the king of Aragon, and to restore unto him his own kingdom of Navarre as a full assurance of peace. Another cometh in with his five eggs, and adviseth to hook in the king of Castile with some hope of affinity or alliance, and to bring to their part certain peers of his court for great pensions. While they all stay at the chiefest doubt of all, what to do in the mean time with England; and yet agree all in this to make peace with the Englishmen, and with most sure and strong bonds to bind that weak and feeble friendship, so that they must be called friends, and had in suspicion as enemies; and that therefore the Scots must be had in a readiness, as it were in a standing, ready at all occasions, in aunters the Englishmen should stir never so little, incontinent to set upon them. And moreover privily and secretly (for openly it may not be done by the truce that is taken), privily, therefore, I say, to make much of some peer of England that is banished his country, which must claim title to the crown of the realm and affirm himself just inheritor thereof, that by this subtle means they may hold to them the king, in whom else they have but small trust and affiance. Here, I say, where so great and high matters be in consultation, where so many noble and wise men counsel their king only to war, here if I, silly man, should rise up and will them to turn over the leaf, and learn a new lesson, saying that my counsel is not to meddle with Italy but to tarry still at home, and that the kingdom of France alone is almost greater than that it may well be governed of one man, so that the king should not need to study how to get more; and then should propose unto them the decrees of the people that be called the Achorians, which be situate over against the island of Utopia on the south-east side.

These Achorians once made war in their king's quarrel for to get him another kingdom which he laid claim unto and advanced himself right inheritor to the crown thereof by the title of an old alliance. At the last, when they had got it, and saw that they had even as much vexation and trouble in keeping it as they had in getting it, and that either their new conquered subjects by sundry occasions were making daily insurrections to rebel against them, or else that other countries were continually with divers inroads and foragings invading them, so that they were ever fighting either for them or against them, and never could break up their camps: seeing themselves in the mean season pilled and impoverished, their money carried out of the realm, their own men killed to maintain the glory of another nation; when they had no war, peace nothing better than war, by reason that their people in war had so inured themselves to corrupt and wicked manners, that they had taken a delight and pleasure in robbing and stealing; that through manslaughter they had gathered boldness to mischief; that their laws were had in contempt, and nothing set by or regarded; that their king, being troubled with the charge and governance of two kingdoms, could not nor was not able perfectly to discharge his office towards them both: seeing again, that all these evils and troubles were endless, at the last [they] laid their heads together, and like faithful and loving subjects gave to their king free choice and liberty to keep still the one of these two kingdoms, whether he would, alleging that he was not able to keep both, and that they were more than might well be governed of half a king, forasmuch as no man would be content to take him for his muleteer that keepeth another man's mules besides his. So this good prince was constrained to be content with his old kingdom and to give over the new to one of his friends. Who shortly after was violently driven out.

Furthermore if I should declare unto them that all this busy preparance to war, whereby so many nations for his sake should be brought into a troublesome hurly-burly, when all his coffers were emptied, his treasures wasted, and his people destroyed, should at the length through some mischance be in vain and to none effect, and that therefore it were best for him to content himself with his own kingdom of France as his forefathers and predecessors did before him, to make much of it, to enrich it, and to make it as flourishing as he could, to endeavour himself to love his subjects and again to be beloved of them, willingly to live with them, peaceably to govern them, and with other kingdoms not to meddle, seeing that which he hath already is even enough for him, yea, and more than he can well turn him to: this mine advice, Master More, how think you it would be heard and taken?

So God help me, not very thankfully, quoth I.

Well, let us proceed then, quoth he. Suppose that some king and his council were together whetting their wits and devising what subtle craft they might invent to enrich the king with great treasures of money. First one counselleth to raise and enhance the valuation of money when the king must pay any, and again to call down the value of coin to less than it is worth when he must receive or gather any. For thus great sums shall be paid with a little money, and where little is due much shall be received. Another counselleth to feign war, that when under this colour and pretence the king hath gathered great abundance of money, he may, when it shall please him, make peace with great solemnity and holy ceremonies, to blind the eyes of the poor community as taking pity and compassion forsooth upon man's blood, like a loving and a merciful prince. Another putteth the king in remembrance of certain old and moth-eaten laws that of long time have not been put in execution, which because no man can remember that they were made, every man hath transgressed. The fines of these laws he counselleth the king to require, for there is no way so profitable nor more honourable as the which hath a shew and colour of justice. Another adviseth him to forbid many things under great penalties and fines, specially such things as is for the people's profit not be used, and afterward to dispense for money with them, which by this prohibition sustain loss and damage. For by this means the favour of the people is won, and profit riseth two ways. First by taking forfeits of them whom covetousness of gains hath brought in danger of this statute, and also by selling privileges and licences, which the better that the prince is, forsooth the dearer he selleth them, as one that is loath to grant to any private person anything that is against the profit of his people, and therefore may sell none but at an exceeding dear price.

Another giveth the king counsel to endanger unto his grace the judges of the realm, that he may have them ever on his side, and that they may in every matter dispute and reason for the king's right; yea, and further to call them into his palace and to require them there to argue and discuss his matters in his own presence. So there shall be no matter of his so openly wrong and unjust wherein one or other of them, either because he will have something to allege and object, or that he is ashamed to say that which is said already, or else to pick a thank with his prince, will not find some hole open to set a snare in, wherewith to take the contrary part in a trip. Thus while the judges cannot agree amongst themselves, reasoning and arguing of that which is plain enough and bringing the manifest truth in doubt, in the mean season the king may take a fit occasion to understand the law as shall most make for his advantage, whereunto all other, for shame or for fear, will agree. Then the judges may be bold to pronounce on the king's side, for he that giveth sentence for the king cannot be without a good excuse. For it shall be sufficient for him to have equity on his part, or the bare words of the law, or a writhen and wrested understanding of the same, or else (which with good and just judges is of greater force than all laws be) the king's indisputable prerogative.

To conclude, all the counsellors agree and consent together with the rich Crassus, that no abundance of gold can be sufficient for a prince which must keep and maintain an army. Furthermore that a king, though he would, can do nothing unjustly; for all that all men have, yea, also the men themselves, be all his. And that every man hath so much of his own as the king's gentleness hath not taken from him. And that it shall be most for the king's advantage that his subjects have very little or nothing in their possession, as whose safeguard doth herein consist, that his people do not wax wanton and wealthy through riches and liberty, because where these things be, there men be not wont patiently to obey hard, unjust, and unlawful commandments; whereas, on the other part, need and poverty doth hold down and keep under stout courages, and maketh them patient perforce, taking from them bold and rebelling stomachs.

Here again, if I should rise up and boldly affirm that all these counsels be to the king dishonour and reproach, whose honour and safety is more and rather supported and upholden by the wealth and riches of his people than by his own treasures; and if I should declare that the commonalty chooseth their king for their own sake, and not for his sake, to the intent that through his labour and study they might all live wealthily safe from wrongs and injuries; and that therefore the king ought to take more care for the wealth of his people than for his own wealth, even as the office and duty of a shepherd is, in that he is a shepherd, to feed his sheep rather than himself.

For as touching this, that they think the defence and maintenance of peace to consist in the poverty of the people, the thing itself sheweth that they be far out of the way. For where shall a man find more wrangling, quarrelling, brawling, and chiding than among beggars? Who be more desirous of new mutations and alterations, than they that be not content with the present state of their life? Or, finally, who be bolder stomached to bring all in a hurly-burly (thereby trusting to get some windfall) than they that have now nothing to lose? And if any king were so smally regarded and so lightly esteemed, yea, so behated of his subjects, that other ways he could not keep them in awe, but only by open wrongs, by polling and shaving and by bringing them to beggary, surely it were better for him to forsake his kingdom than to hold it by this means, whereby though the name of a king be kept, yet the majesty is lost. For it is against the dignity of a king to have rule over beggars, but rather over rich and wealthy men. Of this mind was the hardy and courageous Fabricius when he said that he had rather be a ruler of rich men than be rich himself. And, verily, one man to live in pleasure and wealth while all others weep and smart for it, that is the part, not of a king, but of a jailer. To be short, as he is a foolish physician that cannot cure his patient's disease unless he cast him in another sickness, so he that cannot amend the lives of his subjects but by taking from them the wealth and commodity of life, he must needs grant that he knoweth not the feat how to govern men. But let him rather amend his own life, renounce unhonest pleasures, and forsake pride; for these be the chief vices that cause him to run in the contempt or hatred of his people. Let him live of his own, hurting no man. Let him do cost not above his power. Let him restrain wickedness. Let him prevent vices, and take away the occasions of offences by well ordering his subjects, and not by suffering wickedness to increase, afterwards to be punished. Let him not be too hasty in calling again laws which a custom hath abrogated, specially such as have been long forgotten and never lacked nor needed. And let him never, under the cloak and pretence of transgression, take such fines and forfeits as no judge will suffer a private person to take as unjust and full of guile.

Here if I should bring forth before them the law of the Macarians, which be not far distant from Utopia, whose king the day of his coronation is bound by a solemn oath that he shall never at any time have in his treasury above a thousand pound of gold or silver. They say a very good king, which took more care for the wealth and commodity of his country than for the enriching of himself, made this law to be a stop and a bar to kings from heaping and hoarding up so much money as might impoverish their people. For he foresaw that this sum of treasure would suffice to support the king in battle against his own people if they should chance to rebel, and also to maintain his wars against the invasions of his foreign enemies. Again, he perceived the same stock of money to be too little and insufficient to encourage and enable him wrongfully to take away other men's goods, which was the chief cause why the law was made. Another cause was this: He thought that by this provision his people should not lack money wherewith to maintain their daily occupying and chaffare. And seeing the king could not choose but lay out and bestow all that came in above the prescript sum of his stock, he thought he would seek no occasions to do his subjects injury. Such a king shall be feared of evil men and loved of good men. These, and such other information, if I should use among men wholly inclined and given to the contrary part, how deaf hearers think you should I have?

Deaf hearers doubtless, quoth I, and in good faith no marvel. And to be plain with you, truly I cannot allow that such communication shall be used, or such counsel given, as you be sure shall never be regarded nor received. For how can so strange information be profitable, or how can they be beaten into their heads whose minds be already prevented with clean contrary persuasions? This school philosophy is not unpleasant among friends in familiar communication, but in the councils of kings, where great matters be debated and reasoned with great authority, these things have no place.

That is it which I meant, quoth he, when I said philosophy had no place among kings.

Indeed, quoth I, this school philosophy hath not, which thinketh all things meet for every place. But there is another philosophy more civil, which knoweth, as ye would say, her own stage, and thereafter, ordering and behaving herself in the play that she hath in hand, playeth her part accordingly with comeliness, uttering nothing out of due order and fashion. And this is the philosophy that you must use. Or else whiles a comedy of Plautus is playing, and the vile bondmen scoffing and trifling among themselves, if you should suddenly come upon the stage in a philosopher's apparel, and rehearse out of *Octavia* the place wherein Seneca disputeth with Nero, had it not been better for you to have played the dumb person, than, by rehearsing that which served neither for the time nor place, to have made such a tragical comedy or galli-maufry? For by bringing in other stuff that nothing apper-taineth to the present matter, you must needs mar and pervert the play that is in hand, though the stuff that you bring be much better. What part soever you have taken upon you, play that as well as you can and make the best of it. And do not therefore disturb and bring out of order the whole matter because that another which is merrier and better cometh to your remembrance.

So the case standeth in a commonwealth, and so it is in the consultations of kings and princes. If evil opinions and naughty persuasions cannot be utterly and quite plucked out of their hearts, if you cannot even as you would remedy vices which use and custom hath confirmed, yet for this cause you must not leave and forsake the common-wealth. You must not forsake the ship in a tempest because you cannot rule and keep down the winds. No, nor you must not labour to drive into their heads new and strange information which you know well shall be nothing regarded with them that be of clean contrary minds. But you must with a crafty wile and a subtle train study and endeavour yourself, as much as in you lieth, to handle the matter wittily and handsomely for the purpose; and that which you cannot turn to good, so to order it that it be not very bad. For it is not possible for all things to be well unless all men were good, which I think will not be yet this good many years.

By this means, quoth he, nothing else will be brought to pass, but whiles that I go about to remedy the madness of others I should be even as mad as they. For if I would speak such things that be true I must needs speak such things; but as for to speak false things, whether that be a philosopher's part or no I cannot tell, truly it is not my part. Howbeit, this communication of mine, though per-adventure it may seem unpleasant to them, yet can I not see why it should seem strange or foolishly newfangled. If so be that I should speak those things that Plato feigneth in his weal-public, or that the Utopians do in theirs, these things, though they were (as they be indeed) better, yet they might seem spoken out of place, foras-much as here amongst us every man hath his possessions several to himself, and there all things be common. But what was in my communication contained that might not, and ought not, in any place to be spoken? Saving that to them which have thoroughly decreed and determined with themselves to run headlong the contrary way it can-not be acceptable and pleasant, because it calleth them back and sheweth them the jeopardies. Verily, if all things that evil and vicious manners have caused to seem incon-venient and nought should be refused as things unmeet and reproachful, then we must among Christian people wink at the most part of all those things which Christ taught us and so straitly forbade them to be winked at, that those things also which He whispered in the ears of his disciples He commanded to be proclaimed in open houses. And yet the most part of them is more dissident from the manners of the world nowadays than my communication was.

But preachers, sly and wily men, following your counsel (as I suppose) because they saw men evil willing to frame their manners to Christ's rule, they have wrested and wried His doctrine, and like a rule of lead have applied it to men's manners, that by some means, at the least way, they might agree together. Whereby I cannot see what good they have done, but that men may more securely be evil. And I truly should prevail even as little in kings' councils. For either I must say otherways than they say, and then I were as good to say nothing; or else I must say the same that they say, and (as Mitio saith in Terence), help to further their madness. For that crafty wile and subtle train of yours, I cannot perceive to what purpose it serveth, wherewith you would have me to study and endeavour myself, if all things cannot be made good, yet to handle them wittily and handsomely for the purpose, that as far forth as is possible they may not be very evil. For there is no place to dissemble in nor to wink in. Naughty counsels must be openly allowed and very pestilent decrees must be approved. He shall be counted worse than a spy, yea, almost as evil as a traitor, that with a faint heart doth praise evil and noisome decrees.

Moreover, a man can have no occasion to do good, chancing into the company of them which will sooner pervert a good man than be made good themselves, through whose evil company he shall be marred, or else, if he remain good and innocent, yet the wickedness and folly of others shall be imputed to him and laid in his neck. So that it is impossible with that crafty wile and subtle train to turn anything to better. Wherefore Plato by a goodly similitude declareth why wise men refrain to meddle in the commonwealth. For when they see the

51

people swarm into the streets, and daily wet to the skin with rain, and yet cannot persuade them to go out of the rain and to take their houses, knowing well that if they should go out to them they should nothing prevail nor win aught by it but with them be wet also in the rain, they do keep themselves within their houses, being content that they be safe themselves, seeing they cannot remedy the folly of the people.

Howbeit, doubtless, Master More (to speak truly as my mind giveth me), where possessions be private, where money beareth all the stroke, it is hard and almost impossible that there the weal-public may justly be governed and prosperously flourish. Unless you think thus: that justice is there executed where all things come into the hands of evil men, or that prosperity there flourisheth where all is divided among a few, which few, nevertheless, do not lead their lives very wealthily, and the residue live miserably, wretchedly, and beggarly. Wherefore when I consider with myself and weigh in my mind the wise and godly ordinances of the Utopians, among whom with very few laws all things be so well and wealthily ordered that virtue is had in price and estimation, and yet, all things being there common, every man hath abundance of everything. Again, on the other part, when I compare with them so many nations ever making new laws, yet none of them all well and sufficiently furnished with laws, where every man calleth that he hath gotten his own proper and private goods, where so many new laws daily made be not sufficient for every man to enjoy, defend, and know from another man's that which he calleth his own; which thing the infinite controversies in the law, daily rising, never to be ended, plainly declare to be true: these things (I say) when I consider with myself, I hold well with Plato, and do nothing marvel that he would make no laws for them that refused those laws whereby all men should have and enjoy equal portions of wealths and commodities.

For the wise man did easily foresee this to be the one

and only way to the wealth of a commonalty, if equality
of all things should be brought in and stablished. Which,
I think, is not possible to be observed where every man's
good be proper and peculiar to himself. For where every
man under certain titles and pretences draweth and
plucketh to himself as much as he can, so that a few
divide among themselves all the whole riches, be there
never so much abundance and store, there to the residue
is left lack and poverty. And for the most part it chanceth
that this latter sort is more worthy to enjoy that state of
wealth than the other be, because the rich men be covetous, crafty, and unprofitable. On the other part the poor
be lowly, simple, and by their daily labour more profitable
to the commonwealth than to themselves. Thus I do fully
persuade myself that no equal and just distribution of
things can be made, nor that perfect wealth shall ever be
among men, unless this propriety be exiled and banished.
But so long as it shall continue, so long shall remain
among the most and best part of men the heavy and
inevitable burden of poverty and wretchedness. Which,
as I grant that it may be somewhat eased, so I utterly
deny that it can wholly be taken away. For if there were
a statute made that no man should possess above a certain
measure of ground, and that no man should have in his
stock above a prescript and appointed sum of money, if
it were by certain laws decreed that neither the king
should be of too great power, neither the people too haut
and wealthy, and that offices should not be obtained by
inordinate suit, or by bribes and gifts, that they should
neither be bought nor sold, nor that it should be needful
for the officers to be at any cost or charge in their offices
(for so occasion is given to them by fraud and ravin to
gather up their money again, and by reason of gifts and
bribes the offices be given to rich men, which should
rather have been executed of wise men) by such laws,
I say, like as sick bodies that be desperate and past cure
be wont with continual good cherishing to be kept and
botched up for a time, so these evils also might be

lightened and mitigated. But that they may be perfectly cured, and brought to a good and upright state, it is not to be hoped for, whiles every man is master of his own to himself. Yea, and whiles you go about to do your cure of one part you shall make bigger the sore of another part, so the help of one causeth another's harm, forasmuch as nothing can be given to any one unless it be taken from another.

But I am of a contrary opinion, quoth I, for methinketh that men shall never there live wealthily where all things be common. For how can there be abundance of goods or of anything where every man withdraweth his hand from labour? Whom the regard of his own gains driveth not to work, but the hope that he hath in other men's travails maketh him slothful. Then when they be pricked with poverty, and yet no man can by any law or right defend that for his own which he hath gotten with the labour of his own hands, shall not there of necessity be continual sedition and bloodshed? Specially the authority and reverence of magistrates being taken away, which, what place it may have with such men among whom is no difference, I cannot devise.

I marvel not, quoth he, that you be of this opinion. For you conceive in your mind either none at all, or else a very false image and similitude of this thing. But if you had been with me in Utopia and had presently seen their fashions and laws, as I did which lived there five years and more, and would never have come thence but only to make that new land known here, then doubtless you would grant that you never saw people well ordered but only there.

Surely, quoth Master Peter, it shall be hard for you to make me believe that there is better order in that new land than is here in these countries that we know. For good wits be as well here as there, and I think our commonwealths be ancienter than theirs. Wherein long use and experience hath found out many things commodious for man's life, besides that many things here among us have been found by chance which no wit could ever have devised.

As touching the ancientness, quoth he, of common-wealths, then you might better judge, if you had read the histories and chronicles of that land, which if we may believe, cities were there before men were here. Now what thing soever hitherto by wit hath been devised or found by chance, that might be as well there as here. But I think verily, though it were so that we did pass them in wit, yet in study, in travail, and in laboursome endeavour they far pass us. For (as their chronicles testify) before our arrival there they never heard anything of us whom they call the ultra-equinoctials; saving that once about 1200 years ago, a certain ship was lost by the isle of Utopia which was driven thither by tempest. Certain Romans and Egyptians were cast on land, which after that never went thence. Mark now what profit they took of this one occasion through diligence and earnest travail. There was no craft nor science within the empire of Rome whereof any profit could rise, but they either learned it of these strangers, or else of them taking occasion to search for it, found it out. So great profit was it to them that ever any went thither from hence. But if any like chance before this hath brought any man from thence hither, that is as quite out of remembrance as this also perchance in time to come shall be forgotten, that ever I was there. And like as they quickly, almost at the first meeting, made their own whatsoever is among us wealthily devised, so I suppose it would be long before we would receive any-thing that among them is better instituted than among us. And this, I suppose, is the chief cause why their com-monwealths be wiselier governed and do flourish in more wealth than ours, though we neither in wit nor riches be their inferiors.

Therefore, gentle Master Raphael, quoth I, I pray you and beseech you describe unto us the island. And study not to be short, but declare largely in order their grounds, their rivers, their cities, their people, their manners, their ordinances, their laws, and, to be short, all things that you shall think us desirous to know. And you shall think us desirous to know whatsoever we know not yet.

There is nothing, quoth he, that I will do gladlier. For all these things I have fresh in mind. But the matter requireth leisure.

Let us go in, therefore, quoth I, to dinner; afterward we will bestow the time at our pleasure.

Content, quoth he, be it. So we went in and dined. When dinner was done, we came into the same place again, and sat us down upon the same bench, commanding our servants that no man should trouble us. Then I and Master Peter Giles desired Master Raphael to perform his promise. He, therefore, seeing us desirous and willing to hearken to him, when he had sit still and paused a little while musing and bethinking himself, thus he began to speak.

THE END OF THE FIRST BOOK

THE COMMUNICATION OF
RAPHAEL HYTHLODAY,

*Concerning the best state of a commonwealth
containing the description of Utopia, with a large
declaration of the politic government and of all
the good laws and orders of the same land.*

THE island of Utopia containeth in breadth in the middle
part of it (for there it is broadest) 200 miles. Which
breadth continueth through the most part of the land,
saving that by little and little it cometh in and waxeth
narrower towards both the ends. Which fetching about a
circuit or compass of 500 miles, do fashion the whole
island like to the new moon. Between these two corners
the sea runneth in, dividing them asunder by the distance
of eleven miles or thereabouts, and there surmounteth
into a large and wide sea, which by reason that the land
on every side compasseth it about and sheltereth it from
the winds, is not rough nor mounteth not with great
waves, but almost floweth quietly, not much unlike a
great standing pool, and maketh wellnigh all the space
within the belly of the land in manner of a haven, and to
the great commodity of the inhabitants receiveth in ships
towards every part of the land. The forefronts or frontiers
of the two corners, what with fords and shelves and what
with rocks, be very jeopardous and dangerous. In the
middle distance between them both standeth up above
the water a great rock, which therefore is nothing perilous
because it is in sight. Upon the top of this rock is a fair and
a strong tower builded, which they hold with a garrison of
men. Other rocks there be lying hid under the water,
which therefore be dangerous. The channels be known
only to themselves, and therefore it seldom chanceth that
any stranger, unless be he guided by an Utopian, can
come into this haven, insomuch that they themselves

could scarcely enter without jeopardy, but that their way is directed and ruled by certain landmarks standing on the shore. By turning, translating, and removing these marks into other places they may destroy their enemies' navies, be they never so many. The outside or utter circuit of the land is also full of havens, but the landing is so surely fenced, what by nature and what by workmanship of man's hand, that a few defenders may drive back many armies.

Howbeit, as they say and as the fashion of the place itself doth partly shew, it was not ever compassed about with the sea. But King Utopus, whose name as conqueror the island beareth (for before his time it was called Abraxa), which also brought the rude and wild people to that excellent perfection in all good fashions, humanity, and civil gentleness, wherein they now go beyond all the people of the world, even at his first arriving and entering upon the land, forthwith obtaining the victory, caused fifteen miles space of uplandish ground, where the sea had no passage, to be cut and digged up, and so brought the sea round about the land. He set to this work not only the inhabitants of the island (because they should not think it done in contumely and despite) but also all his own soldiers. Thus the work, being divided into so great a number of workmen, was with exceeding marvellous speed dispatched. Insomuch that the borderers, which at the first began to mock and to jest at this vain enterprise, then turned their derision to marvel at the success and to fear. There be in the island fifty-four large and fair cities, or shire towns, agreeing all together in one tongue, in like manners, institutions, and laws. They be all set and situate alike, and in all points fashioned alike, as far forth as the place or plot suffereth.

Of these cities they that be nighest together be twenty-four miles asunder. Again, there is none of them distant from the next above one day's journey afoot. There come yearly to Amaurote out of every city three old men wise and well experienced, there to entreat and debate of the common matters of the land. For this city (because it standeth just in the midst of the island, and is therefore most meet for the ambassadors of all parts of the realm) is taken for the chief and head city. The precincts and bounds of the shires be so commodiously appointed out and set forth for the cities, that none of them all hath of any side less than twenty miles of ground, and of some side also much more, as of that part where the cities be of farther distance asunder. None of the cities desire to enlarge the bounds and limits of their shires, for they count themselves rather the good husbands than the owners of their lands.

They have in the country, in all parts of the shire, houses or farms builded, well appointed and furnished with all sorts of instruments and tools belonging to husbandry. These houses be inhabited of the citizens which come thither to dwell by course. No household or farm in the country hath fewer than forty persons, men and women, besides two bondmen which be all under the rule and order of the goodman and the goodwife of the house, being both very sage, discreet, and ancient persons. And every thirty farms or families have one head ruler which is called a Philarch, being as it were a head bailiff. Out of every one of these families or farms cometh every year into the city twenty persons which have continued two years before in the country. In their place so many fresh be sent thither out of the city, who, of them that have been there a year already and be therefore expert and cunning in husbandry, shall be instructed and taught. And they the next year shall teach other. This order is used for fear that either scarceness of victuals or some other like incommodity should chance, through lack of knowledge if they should be altogether new and fresh and unexpert in husbandry. This manner and fashion of yearly changing and renewing the occupiers of husbandry, though it be solemn and customably used to the intent that no man shall be constrained against his will to continue long in that hard and sharp kind of life, yet many of them have such a pleasure and delight in husbandry that they obtain a longer space of years. These husbandmen plow and till the ground, and breed up cattle, and provide and make ready wood which they carry to the city either by land or by water as they may most conveniently. They bring up a great multitude of pullen, and that by a marvellous policy. For the hens do not sit upon the eggs, but by keeping them in a certain equal heat they bring life into them and hatch them. The chickens, as soon as they be come out of the shell, follow men and women instead of the hens. They bring up very few horses, nor none but very fierce ones; and that for none other use or purpose, but only to exercise their youth in riding and feats of arms, for oxen be put to all the labour of plowing and drawing. Which they grant to be not so good as horses at a sudden brunt and (as we say) at a dead lift, but yet they hold opinion that oxen will abide and suffer much more labour, pain, and hardness than horses will. And they think that oxen be not in danger and subject unto so many diseases, and that they be kept and maintained with much less cost and charge, and finally that they be good for meat when they be past labour. They sow corn only for bread, for their drink is either wine made of grapes or else of apples or pears, or else it is clear water, and many times mead made of honey or liquorice sodden in water, for thereof they have great store. And though they know certainly (for they know it perfectly indeed) how much victuals the city with the whole country or shire round about it doth spend, yet they sow much more corn and breed up much more cattle than serveth for their own use, parting the overplus among their borderers. Whatsoever necessary things be lacking in the country, all such stuff they fetch out of the city where without any exchange they easily obtain it of the magistrates of the city. For every month many of them go into the city on the holy day. When their harvest day draweth near and is at hand, then the Philarchs, which be the head officers and bailiffs of husbandry, send word to the magistrates of the city what number of harvest men is needful to be sent to them out of the city. The which company of harvest men being ready at the day appointed, almost in one fair day dispatcheth all the harvest work.

Of the cities and namely of Amaurote

As for their cities, whoso knoweth one of them knoweth them all, they be all so like one to another as far forth as the nature of the place permitteth. I will describe, therefore, to you one or other of them, for it skilleth not greatly which, but which rather than Amaurote? Of them all this is the worthiest and of most dignity. For the residue knowledge it for the head city because there is the council house. Nor to me any of them all is better beloved, as wherein I lived five whole years together. The city of Amaurote standeth upon the side of a low hill, in fashion almost four-square. For the breadth of it beginneth a little beneath the top of the hill, and still continueth by the space of two miles until it come to the river of Anyder. The length of it, which lieth by the river's side, is somewhat more. The river of Anyder riseth four and twenty miles above Amaurote out of a little spring, but being increased by other small rivers and brooks that run into it, and among other two somewhat big ones, before the city it is half a mile broad, and farther broader. And forty miles beyond the city it falleth into the ocean sea. By all that space that lieth between the sea and the city, and certain miles also above the city, the water ebbeth and floweth six hours together with a swift tide. When the sea floweth in, for the length of thirty miles it filleth all the Anyder with salt water, and driveth back the fresh water of the river. And somewhat farther it changeth the sweetness of the fresh water with saltness. But a little beyond that the river waxeth sweet, and runneth forby the city fresh and pleasant. And when the sea ebbeth and goeth back again, the fresh water followeth it almost even to the very fall into the sea. There goeth a bridge over the river, made not of piles or of timber, but of stonework with gorgeous and substantial arches at that part of the city that is farthest from the sea, to the intent that ships may pass along forby all the side of the city without let. They have also another river which, indeed, is not very great, but it runneth gently and pleasantly. For it riseth even out of the same hill that the city standeth upon, and runneth down a slope through the midst of the city into Anyder. And because it riseth a little without the city, the Amaurotians have enclosed the head spring of it with strong fences and bulwarks, and so have joined it to the city. This is done to the intent that the water should not be stopped nor turned away or poisoned if their enemies should chance to come upon them. From thence the water is derived and conveyed down in channels of brick divers ways into the lower parts of the city. Where that cannot be done, by reason that the place will not suffer it, there they gather the rain water in great cisterns, which doeth them as good service.

The city is compassed about with a high and thick stone wall full of turrets and bulwarks. A dry ditch, but deep and broad and overgrown with bushes, briars, and thorns, goeth about three sides or quarters of the city. To the fourth side the river itself serveth for a ditch. The streets be appointed and set forth very commodious and handsome, both for carriage and also against the winds. The houses be of fair and gorgeous building, and on the street side they stand joined together in a long row through the whole street without any partition or separation. The streets be twenty foot broad. On the back side of the houses, through the whole length of the street, lie large gardens enclosed round about with the back part of the streets. Every house hath two doors, one into the street, and a postern door on the back side into the garden. These doors be made with two leaves never locked nor bolted, so easy to be opened, that they will follow the least drawing of a finger, and shut again alone. Whoso will may go in, for there is nothing within the houses that is private or any man's own. And every tenth year they change their houses by lot.

They set great store by their gardens. In them they have vineyards, all manner of fruit, herbs, and flowers, so pleasant, so well furnished, and so finely kept, that I never saw thing more fruitful nor better trimmed in any place. Their study and diligence herein cometh not only of pleasure, but also of a certain strife and contention that is between street and street concerning the trimming, husbanding, and furnishing of their gardens, every man for his own part. And verily you shall not lightly find in all the city anything that is more commodious, either for the profit of the citizens or for pleasure. And therefore it may seem that the first founder of the city minded nothing so much as these gardens. For they say that King Utopus himself, even at the first beginning, appointed and drew forth the platform of the city into this fashion and figure that it hath now, but the gallant garnishing and the beautiful setting forth of it, whereunto he saw that one man's age would not suffice, that he left to his posterity. For their chronicles, which they keep written with all diligent circumspection, containing the history of 1760 years, even from the first conquest of the island, record and witness that the houses in the beginning were very low and like homely cottages or poor shepherd houses, made, at all adventures, of every rude piece of timber that came first to hand, with mud walls and ridged roofs thatched over with straw. But now the houses be curiously builded after a gorgeous and gallant sort, with three storeys one over another. The outsides of the walls be made either of hard flint or of plaster, or else of brick, and the inner sides be well strengthened with timber work. The roofs be plain and flat, covered with a certain kind of plaster that is of no cost, and yet so tempered that no fire can hurt or perish it, and withstandeth the violence of the weather better than any lead. They keep the wind out of their windows with glass, for it is there much used, and somewhere also with fine linen cloth dipped in oil or amber, and that for two commodities, for by this means more light cometh in, and the wind is better kept out.

Of the Magistrates

Every thirty families or farms choose them yearly an officer which in their old language is called the Syphogrant, and by a newer name the Philarch. Every ten Syphogrants, with all their thirty families, be under an officer which was once called the Tranibore, now the chief Philarch. Moreover, as concerning the election of the prince, all the Syphogrants, which be in number 200, first be sworn to choose him whom they think most meet and expedient. Then by a secret election they name prince one of those four whom the people before named unto them. For out of the four quarters of the city there be four chosen, out of every quarter one, to stand for the election, which be put up to the council. The prince's office continueth all his lifetime, unless he be deposed or put down for suspicion of tyranny. They choose the Tranibores yearly, but lightly they change them not. All the other officers be but for one year. The Tranibores every third day, and sometimes, if need be, oftener, come into the council house with the prince. Their counsel is concerning the commonwealth. If there be any controversies among the commoners, which be very few, they dispatch and end them by and by. They take ever two Syphogrants to them in council, and every day a new couple. And it is provided that nothing touching the commonwealth shall be confirmed and ratified unless it have been reasoned of and debated three days in the council before it be decreed. It is death to have any consultation for the commonwealth out of the council or the place of the common election. This statute, they say, was made to the intent that the prince and Tranibores might not easily conspire together to oppress the people by tyranny, and to change the state of the weal-public. Therefore matters of great weight and importance be brought to the election house of the Syphogrants, which open the matter to their families and afterward, when they have consulted among themselves, they shew their device to the council. Sometimes the matter is brought before the council of the whole island. Furthermore, this custom also the council useth, to dispute or reason of no matter the same day that it is first proposed or put forth, but to defer it to the next sitting of the council. Because that no man, when he hath rashly there spoken that cometh to his tongue's end, shall then afterward rather study for reasons wherewith to defend and maintain his first foolish sentence, than for the commodity of the commonwealth, as one rather willing the harm or hindrance of the weal-public than any loss or diminution of his own existimation, and as one that would be ashamed (which is a very foolish shame) to be counted anything at the first overseen in the matter. Who at the first ought to have spoken rather wisely than hastily or rashly.

Of Sciences, Crafts, and Occupations

Husbandry is a science common to them all in general, both men and women, wherein they be all expert and cunning. In this they be all instructed even from their youth, partly in their schools with traditions and precepts, and partly in the country nigh the city, brought up, as it were in playing, not only beholding the use of it, but by occasion of exercising their bodies practising it also. Besides husbandry, which (as I said) is common to them all, every one of them learneth one or other several and particular science as his own proper craft. That is most commonly either clothworking in wool or flax, or masonry, or the smith's craft, or the carpenter's science. For there is none other occupation that any number to speak of doth use there. For their garments, which throughout all the island be of one fashion (saving that there is a difference between the man's garment and the woman's, between the married and the unmarried), and this one continueth for evermore unchanged, seemly and comely to the eye, no let to the moving and wielding of the body, also fit both for winter and summer. As for these garments (I say) every family maketh their own. But of the other foresaid crafts every man learneth one, and not only the men, but also the women. But the women, as the weaker sort, be put to the easier crafts, as to work wool and flax; the more laboursome sciences be committed to the men. For the most part every man is brought up in his father's craft, for most commonly they be naturally thereto bent and inclined. But if a man's mind stand to any other, he is by adoption put into a family of that occupation which he doth most fantasy. Whom not only his father but also the magistrates do diligently look to that he be put to a discreet and an honest householder. Yea, and if any person when he hath learned one craft be desirous to learn also another, he is likewise suffered and permitted. When he hath learned both, he occupieth whether he will, unless the city have more need of the one than of the other.

The chief and almost the only office of the Syphogrants is to see and take heed that no man sit idle, but that every one apply his own craft with earnest diligence; and yet for all that, not to be wearied from early in the morning to late in the evening with continual work, like labouring and toiling beasts. For this is worse than the miserable and wretched condition of bondmen, which nevertheless is almost everywhere the life of workmen and artificers, saving in Utopia. For they, dividing the day and the night into twenty-four just hours, appoint and assign only six of those hours to work: three before noon, upon the which they go straight to dinner. And after dinner, when they have rested two hours, then they work three hours, and upon that they go to supper. About eight of the clock in the evening (counting one of the clock at the first hour after noon) they go to bed; eight hours they give to sleep. All the void time that is between the hours of work, sleep, and meat, that they be suffered to bestow, every man as he liketh best himself. Not to the intent that they should misspend this time in riot or slothfulness, but being then licensed from the labour of their own occupations, to bestow the time well and thriftily upon some other science as shall please them. For it is a solemn custom there, to have lectures daily early in the morning, where to be present they only be constrained that be namely chosen and appointed to learning. Howbeit, a great multitude of every sort of people, both men and women, go to hear lectures, some one and some another, as every man's nature is inclined. Yet, this notwithstanding, if any man had rather bestow this time upon his own occupation (as it chanceth in many whose minds rise not in the contemplation of any science liberal), he is not letted nor prohibited, but is also praised and commended as profitable to the commonwealth. After supper they bestow one hour in play, in summer in their gardens, in winter in their common halls where they dine and sup. There they exercise themselves in music, or else in honest and wholesome communication. Dice-play and such other foolish and pernicious games they know not; but they use two games not much unlike the chess. The one is the battle of numbers, wherein one number stealeth away another. The other is wherein vices fight with virtues, as it were in battle array or a set field. In the which game is very properly shewed both the strife and discord that vices have among themselves, and again their unity and concord against virtues; and also what vices be repugnant to what virtues; with what power and strength they assail them openly; by what wiles and subtlety they assault them secretly; with what help and aid the virtues resist and overcome the puissance of the vices; by what craft they frustrate their purposes; and, finally, by what sleight or means the one getteth the victory.

But here lest you be deceived, one thing you must look more narrowly upon. For seeing they bestow but six hours in work, perchance you may think that the lack of some necessary things hereof may ensue. But this is nothing so.

For that small time is not only enough but also too much for the store and abundance of all things that be requisite either for the necessity or commodity of life. The which thing you also shall perceive if you weigh and consider with yourselves how great a part of the people in other countries liveth idle. First, almost all women, which be the half of the whole number, or else, if the women be somewhere occupied, there most commonly in their stead the men be idle. Besides this, how great and how idle a company is there of priests and religious men, as they call them! Put thereto all rich men, specially all landed men, which commonly be called gentlemen and noblemen. Take into this number also their servants, I mean all that flock of stout bragging rushbucklers; join to them also sturdy and valiant beggars, cloaking their idle life under the colour of some disease or sickness, and truly you shall find them much fewer than you thought, by whose labour all these things are wrought that in men's affairs are now daily used and frequented. Now consider with yourself of these few that do work, how few be occupied in necessary works. For where money beareth all the swing, there many vain and superfluous occupations must needs be used, to serve only for riotous superfluity and unhonest pleasure. For the same multitude that now is occupied in work, if they were divided into so few occupations as the necessary use of nature requireth, in so great plenty of things as then of necessity would ensue doubtless the prices would be too little for the artificers to maintain their livings. But if all these that be now busied about unprofit-able occupations, with all the whole flock of them that live idly and slothfully, which consume and waste every one of them more of these things that come by other men's labour than two of the workmen themselves do, if all these (I say) were set to profitable occupations, you easily perceive how little time would be enough, yea, and too much, to store us with all things that may be requisite either for necessity or for commodity, yea, or for pleasure, so that the same pleasure be true and natural.

And this in Utopia the thing itself maketh manifest and plain. For there, in all the city with the whole country or shire adjoining to it, scarcely 500 persons of all the whole number of men and women that be neither too old nor too weak to work be licensed and discharged from labour. Among them be the Syphogrants, who, though they be by the laws exempt and privileged from labour, yet they exempt not themselves, to the intent that they may the rather by their example provoke others to work. The same vacation from labour do they also enjoy to whom the people, persuaded by the commendation of the priests and secret election of the Syphogrants, have given a perpetual licence from labour to learning. But if any one of them prove not according to the expectation and hope of him conceived, he is forthwith plucked back to the company of artificers. And contrariwise, often it chanceth that a handicraftsman doth so earnestly bestow his vacant and spare hours in learning, and through diligence so profiteth therein, that he is taken from his handy occupation and promoted to the company of the learned. Out of this order of the learned be chosen ambassadors, priests, Tranibores, and finally the prince himself, whom they in their old tongue call Barzanes and, by a newer name, Adamus. The residue of the people being neither idle nor yet occupied about unprofitable exercises, it may be easily judged in how few hours how much good work by them may be done and dispatched towards those things that I have spoken of.

This commodity they have also above other, that in the most part of necessary occupations they need not so much work as other nations do. For, first of all, the building or repairing of houses asketh everywhere so many men's continual labour, because that the unthrifty here suffereth the houses that his father builded in continuance of time to fall in decay. So that which he might have upholden with little cost, his successor is constrained to build it again anew, to his great charge. Yea, many times also the house that stood one man in much money, another is of so nice and so delicate a mind, that he setteth nothing by it; and, it being neglected and therefore shortly falling into ruin, he buildeth up another in another place with no less cost and charge. But among the Utopians, where all things be set in a good order and the commonwealth in a good stay, it very seldom chanceth that they choose a new plot to build an house upon. And they do not only find speedy and quick remedies for present faults, but also prevent them that be like to fall. And by this means their houses continue and last very long with little labour and small reparations; insomuch that this kind of workmen sometimes have almost nothing to do, but that they be commanded to hew timber at home, and to square and trim up stones, to the intent that if any work chance it may the speedlier rise.

Now, sir, in their apparel mark (I pray you) how few workmen they need. First of all, whiles they be at work they be covered homely with leather or skins that will last seven years. When they go forth abroad they cast upon them a cloak which hideth the other homely apparel. These cloaks throughout the whole island be all of one colour, and that is the natural colour of the wool. They therefore do not only spend much less woollen cloth than is spent in other countries, but also the same standeth them in much less cost. But linen cloth is made with less labour, and is therefore had more in use. But in linen cloth only whiteness, in woollen only cleanliness, is regarded. As for the smallness or fineness of the thread, that is nothing passed for. And this is the cause wherefore in other places four or five cloth gowns of divers colours and as many silk coats be not enough for one man. Yea, and if he be of the delicate and nice sort ten be too few, whereas there one garment will serve a man most commonly two years. For why should he desire more, seeing if he had them he should not be the better hapt or covered from cold, neither in his apparel any whit the comelier? Wherefore, seeing they be all exercised in profitable occupations, and that few artificers in the same crafts be sufficient, this is the cause that, plenty of all things being among them, they do sometimes bring forth an innumerable company of people to amend the highways if any be broken. Many times also, when they have no such work to be occupied about, an open proclamation is made that they shall bestow fewer hours in work. For the magistrates do not exercise their citizens against their wills in unneedful labours. For why, in the institution of that weal-public this end is only and chiefly pretended and minded, that what time may possibly be spared from the necessary occupations and affairs of the commonwealth, all that the citizens should withdraw from the bodily service to the free liberty of the mind and garnishing of the same. For herein they suppose the felicity of this life to consist.

Of their Living and Mutual Conversation together

But now will I declare how the citizens use themselves one towards another, what familiar occupying and entertainment there is among the people, and what fashion they use in the distribution of everything. First, the city consisteth of families; the families most commonly be made of kindreds. For the women, when they be married at a lawful age, they go into their husbands' houses, but the male children, with all the whole male offspring, continue still in their own family and be governed of the eldest and ancientest father, unless he dote for age, for then the next to him in age is placed in his room. But to the intent the prescript number of the citizens should neither decrease nor above measure increase, it is ordained that no family, which in every city be six thousand in the whole besides them of the country, shall at once have fewer children of the age of fourteen years or thereabout than ten or more than sixteen, for of children under this age no number can be prescribed or appointed. This measure or number is easily observed and kept by putting them that in fuller families be above the number into families of smaller increase. But if chance be that in the whole city the store increase above the just number, therewith they fill up the lack of other cities. But if so be that the multitude throughout the whole island pass and exceed the due number, then they choose out of every city certain citizens, and build up a town under their own laws in the next land where the inhabitants have much waste and unoccupied ground, receiving also of the same country people to them, if they will join and dwell with them. They thus joining and dwelling together do easily agree in one fashion of living, and that to the great wealth of both the peoples. For they so bring the matter about by their laws, that the ground which before was neither good nor profitable for the one nor for the other is now sufficient and fruitful enough for them both. But if the inhabitants of that land will not dwell with them to be ordered by their laws, then they drive them out of those bounds which they have limited and appointed out for themselves. And if they resist and rebel, then they make war against them. For they count this the most just cause of war, when any people holdeth a piece of ground void and vacant to no good nor profitable use, keeping others from the use and possession of it which notwithstanding by the law of nature ought thereof to be nourished and relieved. If any chance do so much diminish the number of any of their cities that it cannot be filled up again without the diminishing of the just number of the other cities (which they say chanced but twice since the beginning of the land through a great pestilent plague), then they fulfil and make up the number with citizens fetched out of their own foreign towns; for they had rather suffer their foreign towns to decay and perish than any city of their own island to be diminished.

But now again to the conversation of the citizens among themselves. The eldest (as I said) ruleth the family. The wives be ministers to their husbands, the children to their parents, and, to be short, the younger to their elders. Every city is divided into four equal parts or quarters. In the midst of every quarter there is a market-place of all manner of things. Thither the works of every family be brought into certain houses, and every kind of thing is laid up several in barns or storehouses. From hence the father of every family or every householder fetcheth whatsoever he and his have need of, and carrieth it away with him without money, without exchange, without any gage, pawn, or pledge. For why should anything be denied unto him, seeing there is abundance of all things, and that it is not to be feared lest any man will ask more than he needeth? For why should it be thought that that man would ask more than enough which is sure never to lack? Certainly in all kinds of living creatures either fear of lack doth cause covetousness and ravin, or in man only pride, which counteth it a glorious thing to pass and excel other in the superfluous and vain ostentation of things. The which kind of vice among the Utopians can have no place.

Next to the market-places that I spake of stand meat markets, whither be brought not only all sorts of herbs and the fruits of trees, with bread, but also fish, and all manner of four-footed beasts and wild fowl that be man's meat. But first the filthiness and ordure thereof is clean washed away in the running river without the city in places appointed meet for the same purpose. From thence the beasts be brought in, killed, and clean washed by the hands of their bondmen. For they permit not their free citizens to accustom themselves to the killing of beasts, through the use whereof they think clemency, the gentlest affection of our nature, by little and little to decay and perish. Neither they suffer anything that is filthy, loathsome, or uncleanly to be brought into the city, lest the air, by the stench thereof infected and corrupt, should cause pestilent diseases.

Moreover, every street hath certain great large halls set in equal distance one from another, every one known by a several name. In these halls dwell the Syphogrants, and to every one of the same halls be appointed thirty families, on either side fifteen. The stewards of every hall at a certain hour come in to the meat markets, where they receive meat according to the number of their halls. But first and chiefly of all, respect is had to the sick that be cured in the hospitals. For in the circuit of the city, a little without the walls, they have four hospitals, so big, so wide, so ample, and so large, that they may seem four little towns, which were devised of that bigness partly to the intent the sick, be they never so many in number, should not lie too throng or strait, and therefore uneasily and incommodiously; and partly that they which were taken and holden with contagious diseases, such as be wont by infection to creep from one to another, might be laid apart far from the company of the residue. These hospitals be so well appointed, and with all things necessary to health so furnished, and, moreover, so diligent attendance through the continual presence of cunning physicians is given, that though no man be sent thither against his will, yet notwithstanding there is no sick person in all the city that had not rather lie there than at home in his own house. When the steward of the sick hath received such meat as the physicians have prescribed, then the best is equally divided among the halls, according to the company of every one, saving that there is had a respect to the prince, the bishop, the Tranibores, and to ambassadors and all strangers, if there be any, which be very few and seldom. But they also, when they be there, have certain several houses appointed and prepared for them. To these halls at the set hours of dinner and supper cometh all the whole Syphogranty or ward, warned by the noise of a brazen trumpet, except such as be sick in the hospitals, or else in their own houses. Howbeit, no man is prohibited or forbid, after the halls be served, to fetch home meat out of the market to his own house, for they know that no man will do it without a cause reasonable. For though no man be prohibited to dine at home, yet no man doth it willingly because it is counted a point of small honesty. And also it were a folly to take the pain to dress a bad dinner at home, when they may be welcome to good and fine fare so nigh hand at the hall.

In this hall all vile service, all slavery and drudgery, with all laboursome toil and base business, is done by bondmen. But the women of every family, by course, have the office and charge of cookery for seething and dressing the meat and ordering all things thereto belonging. They sit at three tables or more, according to the number of their company. The men sit upon the bench next the wall, and the women against them on the other side of the table, that if any sudden evil should chance to them, as many times happeneth to women with child, they may rise without trouble or disturbance of anybody, and go thence into the nursery.

The nurses sit several alone with their young sucklings in a certain parlour appointed and deputed to the same purpose, never without fire and clean water, nor yet without cradles, that when they will they may lay down the young infants, and at their pleasure take them out of their swathing clothes, and hold them to the fire, and refresh them with play. Every mother is nurse to her own child unless either death or sickness be the let. When that chanceth, the wives of the Syphogrants quickly provide a nurse; and that is not hard to be done, for they that can do it proffer themselves to no service so gladly as to that, because that there this kind of pity is much praised, and the child that is nourished ever after taketh his nurse for his own natural mother. Also among the nurses sit all the children that be under the age of five years. All the other children of both kinds as well boys as girls, that be under the age of marriage, do either serve at the tables or else, if they be too young thereto, yet they stand by with marvellous silence. That which is given to them from the table they eat, and other several dinner time they have none.

The Syphogrant and his wife sit in the midst of the high table, forasmuch as that is counted the honourablest place, and because from thence all the whole company is in their sight. For that table standeth overthwart the over end of the hall. To them be joined two of the ancientest and eldest, for at every table they sit four at a mess. But if there be a church standing in that Syphogranty or ward, then the priest and his wife sitteth with the Syphogrant, as chief in the company. On both sides of them sit young men, and next unto them again old men. And thus throughout all the house equal of age be set together, and yet be mixed and matched with unequal ages. This, they say, was ordained to the intent that the sage gravity and reverence of the elders should keep the youngers from wanton licence of words and behaviour, forasmuch as nothing can be so secretly spoken or done at the table, but either they that sit on the one side or on the other must needs perceive it. The dishes be not set down in order from the first place, but all the old men (whose places be marked with some special token to be known) be first served of their meat, and then the residue equally. The old men divide their dainties as they think best to the younger on each side of them. Thus the elders be not defrauded of their due honour, and nevertheless equal commodity cometh to every one.

They begin every dinner and supper of reading something that pertaineth to good manners and virtue; but it is short, because no man shall be grieved therewith. Hereof the elders take occasion of honest communication, but neither sad nor unpleasant. Howbeit, they do not spend all the whole dinner time themselves with long and tedious talks, but they gladly hear also the young men, yea, and purposely provoke them to talk, to the intent that they may have a proof of every man's wit and towardness or disposition to virtue, which commonly in the liberty of feasting doth shew and utter itself. Their dinners be very short, but their suppers be somewhat longer, because that after dinner followeth labour, after supper sleep and natural rest, which they think to be of more strength and efficacy to wholesome and healthful digestion. No supper is passed without music, nor their banquets lack no conceits nor junkets. They burn sweet gums and spices or perfumes and pleasant smells, and sprinkle about sweet ointments and waters, yea, they leave nothing undone that maketh for the cheering of the company. For they be much inclined to this opinion, to think no kind of pleasure forbidden whereof cometh no harm. Thus, therefore, and after this sort they live together in the city; but in the country they that dwell alone far from any neighbours do dine and sup at home in their own houses. For no family there lacketh any kind of victuals, as from whom cometh all that the citizens eat and live by.

Of their Journeying or Travelling abroad, with divers other Matters cunningly Reasoned and wittily Discussed

But if any be desirous to visit either their friends dwelling in another city or to see the place itself, they easily obtain licence of their Syphogrants and Tranibores, unless there be some profitable let. No man goeth out alone, but a company is sent forth together with their prince's letters, which do testify that they have licence to go that journey and prescribeth also the day of their return. They have a wagon given them with a common bondman which driveth the oxen and taketh charge of them. But unless they have women in their company, they send home the wagon again as an impediment and a let. And though they carry nothing forth with them, yet in all their journey they lack nothing, for wheresoever they come they be at home. If they tarry in a place longer than one day, then there every one of them falleth to his own occupation, and be very gently entertained of the workmen and companies of the same crafts. If any man, of his own head and without leave, walk out of his precinct and bounds, taken without the prince's letters he is brought again for a fugitive or a runaway with great shame and rebuke, and is sharply punished. If he be taken in that fault again, he is punished with bondage. If any be desirous to walk abroad

into the fields or into the country that belongeth to the
same city that he dwelleth in, obtaining the goodwill of
his father and the consent of his wife, he is not prohibited.
But into what part of the country soever he cometh he
hath no meat given him until he have wrought out his
forenoon's task or dispatched so much work as there is
wont to be wrought before supper. Observing this law and
condition, he may go whither he will within the bounds of
his own city; for he shall be no less profitable to the city
than if he were within it. Now you see how little liberty
they have to loiter, how they can have no cloak or pretence to idleness. There be neither wine-taverns, nor ale-
houses, nor stews, nor any occasion of vice or wickedness,
no lurking corners, no places of wicked councils or unlawful assemblies. But they be in the present sight and under
the eyes of every man. So that of necessity they must
either apply their accustomed labours, or else recreate
themselves with honest and laudable pastimes.

   This fashion and trade of life being used among the
people, it cannot be chosen but that they must of necessity have store and plenty of all things. And seeing they
be all thereof partners equally, therefore can no man there
be poor or needy. In the council of Amaurote, whither, as
I said, every city sendeth three men apiece yearly, as soon
as it is perfectly known of what things there is in every
place plenty, and again what things be scant in any place,
incontinent the lack of the one is performed and filled up
with the abundance of the other. And this they do freely
without any benefit, taking nothing again of them to
whom the things is given, but those cities that have given
of their store to any other city that lacketh, requiring
nothing again of the same city, do take such things as
they lack of another city to the which they gave nothing.
So the whole island is as it were one family or household.
But when they have made sufficient provision of store for
themselves (which they think not done until they have
provided for two years following, because of the uncertainty of the next year's proof), then of those things

whereof they have abundance they carry forth into other countries great plenty: as grain, honey, wool, flax, wood, madder, purple-dyed fells, wax, tallow, leather, and living beasts. And the seventh part of all these things they give frankly and freely to the poor of that country. The residue they sell at a reasonable and mean price. By this trade of traffic or merchandise they bring into their own country not only great plenty of gold and silver, but also all such things as they lack at home, which is almost nothing but iron. And by reason they have long used this trade, now they have more abundance of these things than any men will believe.

Now, therefore, they care not whether they sell for ready money, or else upon trust to be paid at a day and to have the most part in debts. But in so doing they never follow the credence of private men, but the assurance or warrantise of the whole city by instruments and writings made in that behalf accordingly. When the day of payment is come and expired, the city gathereth up the debt of the private debtors and putteth it into the common box, and so long hath the use and profit of it until the Utopians, their creditors, demand it. The most part of it they never ask, for that thing which is to them no profit to take it from other to whom it is profitable, they think it no right nor conscience. But if the case so stand that they must lend part of that money to another people, then they require their debt, or when they have war. For the which purpose only they keep at home all the treasure which they have, to be helpen and succoured by it either in extreme jeopardies, or in sudden dangers, but especially and chiefly to hire therewith, and that for unreasonable great wages, strange soldiers. For they had rather put strangers in jeopardy than their own countrymen, knowing that for money enough their enemies themselves many times may be bought or sold, or else through treason be set together by the ears among themselves. For this cause they keep an inestimable treasure, but yet not as a treasure, but so they have it and use it, as in good faith

I am ashamed to shew, fearing that my words shall not be believed. And this I have more cause to fear, for that I know how difficult and hardly I myself would have believed another man telling the same, if I had not presently seen it with mine own eyes.

For it must needs be that how far a thing is dissonant and disagreeing from the guise and trade of the hearers, so far shall it be out of their belief. Howbeit, a wise and indifferent esteemer of things will not greatly marvel perchance, seeing all their other laws and customs do so much differ from ours, if the use also of gold and silver among them be applied rather to their own fashions than to ours. I mean, in that they occupy not money themselves, but keep it for that chance which, as it may happen, so it may be that it shall never come to pass. In the meantime gold and silver, whereof money is made, they do so use as none of them doth more esteem it than the very nature of the thing deserveth. And then who doth not plainly see how far it is under iron, as without the which men can no better live than without fire and water? Whereas to gold and silver nature hath given no use that we may not well lack if that the folly of men had not set it in higher estimation for the rareness' sake. But of the contrary part, nature, as a most tender and loving mother, hath placed the best and most necessary things open abroad, as the air, the water, and the earth itself, and hath removed and hid farthest from us vain and unprofitable things. Therefore if these metals among them should be fast locked up in some tower, it might be suspected that the prince and the council (as the people is ever foolishly imagining) intended by some subtlety to deceive the commons and to take some profit of it to themselves. Furthermore, if they should make thereof plate and such other finely and cunningly wrought stuff, if at any time they should have occasion to break it and melt it again, therewith to pay their soldiers' wages, they see and perceive very well that men would be loath to part from those things, that they once began to have pleasure and delight in. To remedy all this they have found out a means which, as it is agreeable to all their other laws and customs, so it is from ours (where gold is so much set by and so diligently kept) very far discrepant and repugnant, and therefore incredible, but only to them that be wise. For whereas they eat and drink in earthen and glass vessels which, indeed, be curiously and properly made and yet be of very small value, of gold and silver they make commonly chamber-pots and other vessels that serve for most vile uses not only in their common halls but in every man's private house. Furthermore, of the same metals they make great chains, fetters, and gyves wherein they tie their bondmen. Finally whosoever for any offence be infamed, by their ears hang rings of gold, upon their fingers they wear rings of gold, and about their necks chains of gold, and, in conclusion, their heads be tied about with gold. Thus by all means possible they procure to have gold and silver among them in reproach and infamy. And these metals, which other nations do as grievously and sorrowfully forgo, as in a manner their own lives, if they should altogether at once be taken from the Utopians, no man there would think that he had lost the worth of one farthing. They gather also pearls by the seaside, and diamonds and carbuncles upon certain rocks; and yet they seek not for them, but by chance finding them, they cut and polish them, and therewith they deck their young infants. Which, like as in the first years of their childhood they make much and be fond and proud of such ornaments, so when they be a little more grown in years and discretion, perceiving that none but children do wear such toys and trifles, they lay them away even of their own shamefastness, without any bidding of their parents, even as our children, when they wax big, do cast away nuts, brooches, and puppets. Therefore these laws and customs, which be so far different from all other nations, how divers fantasies also and minds they do cause, did I never so plainly perceive as in the ambassadors of the Anemolians.

These ambassadors came to Amaurote while I was
there. And because they came to entreat of great and
weighty matters, those three citizens apiece out of every
city were come thither before them. But all the ambassadors of the next countries, which had been there before
and knew the fashions and manners of the Utopians,
among whom they perceived no honour given to sumptuous apparel, silks to be condemned, gold also to be
infamed and reproachful, were wont to come thither in
very homely and simple array. But the Anemolians,
because they dwell far thence and had very little acquaintance with them, hearing that they were all apparelled
alike, and that very rudely and homely, thinking them not
to have the things which they did not wear, being therefore more proud than wise, determined in the gorgeousness of their apparel to represent very gods, and with
the bright shining and glistering of their gay clothing to
dazzle the eyes of the silly poor Utopians. So there came
in three ambassadors with an hundred servants all apparelled in changeable colours, the most of them in silks. The
ambassadors themselves (for at home in their own country
they were noblemen) in cloth of gold, with great chains of
gold, with gold hanging at their ears, with gold rings upon
their fingers, with brooches and aglets of gold upon their
caps which glistered full of pearls and precious stones, to
be short, trimmed and adorned with all those things which
among the Utopians were either the punishment of bondmen or the reproach of infamed persons or else trifles for
young children to play withal.

Therefore it would have done a man good at his heart
to have seen how proudly they displayed their peacock's
feathers, how much they made of their painted sheaths,
and how loftily they set forth and advanced themselves
when they compared their gallant apparel with the poor
raiment of the Utopians. For all the people were swarmed
forth into the streets. And on the other side it was no less
pleasure to consider how much they were deceived and
how far they missed of their purpose, being contrarywise

taken than they thought they should have been. For to the eyes of all the Utopians, except very few which had been in other countries for some reasonable cause, all that gorgeousness of apparel seemed shameful and reproachful. Insomuch that they most reverently saluted the vilest and most abject of them for lords, passing over the ambassadors themselves without any honour, judging them by their wearing of golden chains to be bondmen. Yea, you should have seen children also that had cast away their pearls and precious stones, when they saw the like sticking upon the ambassadors' caps, dig and push their mothers under the sides, saying thus to them: Look, mother, how great a lubber doth yet wear pearls and precious stones as though he were a little child still. But the mother, yea and that also in good earnest, Peace, son, saith she, I think he be some of the ambassadors' fools. Some found fault at their golden chains as to no use nor purpose, being so small and weak that a bondman might easily break them, and again so wide and large, that when it pleased him he might cast them off and run away at liberty whither he would. But when the ambassadors had been there a day or two and saw so great abundance of gold so lightly esteemed, yea, in no less reproach than it was with them in honour, and, besides that, more gold in the chains and gyves of one fugitive bondman than all the costly ornaments of them three was worth, they began to abate their courage, and for very shame laid away all that gorgeous array whereof they were so proud, and specially when they had talked familiarly with the Utopians, and had learned all their fashions and opinions.

For they marvel that any men be so foolish as to have delight and pleasure in the doubtful glistering of a little trifling stone, which may behold any of the stars, or else the sun itself. Or that any man is so mad as to count himself the nobler for the smaller or finer thread of wool, which selfsame wool (be it now in never so fine a spun thread) a sheep did once wear, and yet was she all that time no other thing than a sheep. They marvel also

that gold, which of its own nature is a thing so unprofitable, is now among all people in so high estimation, that
man himself, by whom, yea, and for the use of whom, it
is so much set by, is in much less estimation than the gold
itself. Insomuch that a lumpish blockheaded churl, and
which hath no more wit than an ass, yea, and as full of
naughtiness as of folly, shall have nevertheless many wise
and good men in subjection and bondage only for this,
because he hath a great heap of gold. Which if it should
be taken from him by any fortune or by some subtle wile
and cautel of the law (which no less than fortune doth
both raise up the low and pluck down the high) and be
given to the most vile slave and abject drivel of all his
household, then shortly after he shall go into the service
of his servant, as an augmentation or overplus beside his
money. But they much more marvel at and detest the
madness of them which to those rich men, in whose debt
and danger they be not, do give almost divine honours
for none other consideration but because they be rich,
and yet knowing them to be such niggish penny-fathers,
that they be sure as long as they live not the worth of one
farthing of that heap of gold shall come to them.

These and suchlike opinions have they conceived,
partly by education, being brought up in that commonwealth whose laws and customs be far different from
these kinds of folly, and partly by good literature and
learning. For though there be not many in every city
which be exempt and discharged of all other labours and
appointed only to learning (that is to say, such in whom,
even from their very childhood, they have perceived a
singular towardness, a fine wit, and a mind apt to good
learning), yet all in their childhood be instruct in learning.
And the better part of the people, both men and women,
throughout all their whole life do bestow in learning
those spare hours which we said they have vacant from
bodily labours. They be taught learning in their own
native tongue. For it is both copious in words and also
pleasant to the ear, and for the utterance of a man's mind

very perfect and sure. The most part of all that side of the world useth the same language, saving that among the Utopians it is finest and purest, and according to the diversity of the countries it is diversely altered. Of all these philosophers whose names be here famous in this part of the world to us known, before our coming thither not as much as the fame of any of them was common among them. And yet in music, logic, arithmetic, and geometry they have found out in a manner all that our ancient philosophers have taught.

But as they in all things be almost equal to our old ancient clerks, so our new logicians in subtle inventions have far passed and gone beyond them. For they have not devised one of all those rules of restrictions, amplifications, and suppositions, very wittily invented in the small logicals which here our children in every place do learn. Furthermore, they were never yet able to find out the second intentions, insomuch that none of them all could ever see man himself in common, as they call him, though he be (as you know) bigger than ever was any giant, yea, and pointed to of us even with our finger.

But they be in the course of the stars and the movings of the heavenly spheres very expert and cunning. They have also wittily excogitated and devised instruments of divers fashions, wherein is exactly comprehended and contained the movings and situations of the sun, the moon, and of all the other stars which appear in their horizon. But as for the amities and dissensions of the planets, and all that deceitful divination by the stars, they never as much as dreamed thereof. Rains, winds, and other courses of tempest they know before by certain tokens which they have learned by long use and observation. But of the causes of all these things and of the ebbing, flowing, and saltness of the sea, and finally of the original beginning and nature of heaven and of the world, they hold partly the same opinions that our old philosophers hold, and partly, as our philosophers vary among themselves, so they also, while they bring new reasons of things, do disagree from all them, and yet among themselves in all points they do not accord.

In that part of philosophy which entreateth of manners and virtue their reasons and opinions agree with ours. They dispute of the good qualities of the soul, of the body, and of fortune, and whether the name of goodness may be applied to all these or only to the endowments and gifts of the soul. They reason of virtue and pleasure; but the chief and principal question is in what thing, be it one or more, the felicity of man consisteth. But in this point they seem almost too much given and inclined to the opinion of them which defend pleasure, wherein they determine either all or the chiefest part of man's felicity to rest. And (which is more to be marvelled at) the defence of this so dainty and delicate an opinion they fetch even from their grave, sharp, bitter, and rigorous religion. For they never dispute of felicity or blessedness but they join unto the reasons of philosophy certain principles taken out of religion, without the which to the investigation of true felicity they think reason of itself weak and unperfect. Those principles be these and suchlike: That the soul is immortal, and by the bountiful goodness of God ordained to felicity. That to our virtues and good deeds rewards be appointed after this life, and to our evil deeds punishments. Though these be pertaining to religion, yet they think it meet that they should be believed and granted by proofs of reason. But if these principles were condemned and disannulled, then without any delay they pronounce no man to be so foolish which would not do all his diligence and endeavour to obtain pleasure by right or wrong, only avoiding this inconvenience, that the less pleasure should not be a let or hindrance to the bigger, or that he laboured not for that pleasure which would bring after it displeasure, grief, and sorrow. For they judge it extreme madness to follow sharp and painful virtue, and not only to banish the pleasure of life, but also willingly to suffer grief, without any hope of profit thereof ensuing. For what profit can there

be if a man, when he hath passed over all his life unpleas-
antly, that is to say, miserably, shall have no reward after
his death?

But now, sir, they think not felicity to rest in all pleasure, but only in that pleasure that is good and honest, and
that hereto as to perfect blessedness our nature is allured
and drawn even of virtue, whereto only they that be of
the contrary opinion do attribute felicity. For they define
virtue to be life ordered according to nature, and that we
be hereunto ordained of God. And that he doth follow
the course of nature, which in desiring and refusing things
is ruled by reason. Furthermore, that reason doth chiefly
and principally kindle in men the love and veneration of
the Divine Majesty of whose goodness it is that we be,
and that we be in possibility to attain felicity. And that
secondarily it both stirreth and provoketh us to lead our
life out of care in joy and mirth, and also moveth us to
help and further all other in respect of the society of
nature to obtain and enjoy the same.

For there was never man so earnest and painful a fol-
lower of virtue and hater of pleasure, that would so enjoin
you labours, watchings, and fastings, but he would also
exhort you to ease, lighten, and relieve, to your power,
the lack and misery of others, praising the same as a deed
of humanity and pity. Then, if it be a point of humanity
for man to bring health and comfort to man, and specially
(which is a virtue most peculiarly belonging to man) to
mitigate and assuage the grief of others, and by taking
from them the sorrow and heaviness of life to restore
them to joy, that is to say, to pleasure, why may it not
then be said that nature doth provoke every man to do
the same to himself? For a joyful life, that is to say, a
pleasant life, is either evil; and if it be so, then thou
shouldest not only help no man thereto, but rather, as
much as in thee lieth, withdraw all men from it as noisome
and hurtful; or else if thou not only mayst, but also of
duty art bound, to procure it to other, why not chiefly to
thyself to whom thou art bound to shew as much favour

and gentleness as to other? For when nature biddeth thee to be good and gentle to other she commandeth thee not to be cruel and ungentle to thyself. Therefore even very nature (say they) prescribeth to us a joyful life, that is to say, pleasure, as the end of all our operations. And they define virtue to be life ordered according to the prescript of nature.

But in that that nature doth allure and provoke men one to help another to live merrily (which surely she doth not without a good cause, for no man is so far above the lot of man's state or condition, that nature doth cark and care for him only which equally favoureth all that be comprehended under the communion of one shape, form, and fashion), verily she commandeth thee to use diligent circumspection, that thou do not so seek for thine own commodities, that thou procure others' incommodities. Wherefore their opinion is, that not only covenants and bargains made among private men ought to be well and faithfully fulfilled, observed, and kept, but also common laws, which either a good prince hath justly published, or else the people, neither oppressed with tyranny, neither deceived by fraud and guile, hath by their common consent constituted and ratified concerning the partition of the commodities of life, that is to say, the matter of pleasure. These laws not offended, it is wisdom that thou look to thine own wealth. And to do the same for the commonwealth is no less than thy duty, if thou bearest any reverent love or any natural zeal and affection to thy native country. But to go about to let another man of his pleasure whiles thou procurest thine own, that is open wrong. Contrariwise, to withdraw something from thyself to give to others, that is a point of humanity and gentleness, which never taketh away so much commodity as it bringeth again. For it is recompensed with the return of benefits; and the conscience of the good deed, with the remembrance of the thankful love and benevolence of them to whom thou hast done it, doth bring more pleasure to thy mind than that which thou hast withholden from thyself could have brought to thy body. Finally (which to a godly-disposed and a religious mind is easy to be persuaded), God recompenseth the gift of a short and small pleasure with great and everlasting joy.

Therefore, the matter diligently weighed and considered, thus they think, that all our actions, and in them the virtues themselves, be referred at the last to pleasure as their end and felicity. Pleasure they call every motion and state of the body or mind wherein man hath naturally delectation. Appetite they join to nature, and that not without a good cause. For like as not only the senses, but also right reason, coveteth whatsoever is naturally pleasant, so that it may be gotten without wrong or injury, not letting or debarring a greater pleasure nor causing painful labour, even so those things that men by vain imagination do feign against nature to be pleasant (as though it lay in their power to change the things, as they do the names of things), all such pleasures they believe to be of so small help and furtherance to felicity, that they count them a great let and hindrance. Because that in whom they have once taken place, all his mind they possess with a false opinion of pleasure, so that there is no place left for true and natural delectations. For there be many things which of their own nature contain no pleasantness, yea, the most part of them much grief and sorrow; and yet, through the perverse and malicious flickering enticements of lewd and unhonest desires, be taken not only for special and sovereign pleasures, but also be counted among the chief causes of life.

In this counterfeit kind of pleasure they put them that I spake of before, which, the better gowns they have on, the better men they think themselves. In the which thing they do twice err, for they be no less deceived in that they think their gown the better, than they be in that they think themselves the better. For if you consider the profitable use of the garment, why should wool of a finer-spun thread be thought better than the wool of a coarse-spun thread? Yet they, as though the one did pass the other by nature and not by their mistaking, advance themselves, and think the price of their own persons thereby greatly increased. And therefore the honour which in a coarse gown they durst not have looked for, they require, as it were of duty, for their finer gown's sake. And if they be passed by without reverence, they take it displeasantly and disdainfully. And again, is it not like madness to take a pride in vain and unprofitable honours? For what natural or true pleasure dost thou take of another man's bare head or bowed knees? Will this ease the pain of thy knees or remedy the frenzy of thy head? In this image of counterfeit pleasure they be of a marvellous madness, which for the opinion of nobility rejoice much in their own conceit, because it was their fortune to come of such ancestors whose stock of long time hath been counted rich (for now nobility is nothing else), specially rich in lands. And though their ancestors left them not one foot of land, or else they themselves have pissed it against the walls, yet they think themselves not the less noble therefore of one hair.

In this number also they count them that take pleasure and delight (as I said) in gems and precious stones, and think themselves almost gods if they chance to get an excellent one, specially of that kind which in that time of their own countrymen is had in highest estimation. For one kind of stone keepeth not his price still in all countries and at all times. Nor they buy them not, but taken out of the gold and bare; no nor so neither, until they have made the seller to swear that he will warrant and assure it to be a true stone and no counterfeit gem. Such care they take lest a counterfeit stone should deceive their eyes instead of a right stone. But why shouldest thou not take even as much pleasure in beholding a counterfeit stone, which thine eye cannot discern from a right stone? They should both be of like value to thee, even as to the blind man. What shall I say of them that keep superfluous riches, to take delectation only in the beholding and not in the use or occupying thereof? Do they take true pleasure, or else be they deceived with false pleasure? Or of them that be in a contrary vice, hiding the gold which they shall never occupy, nor peradventure never see more? And whiles they take care lest they shall lose it, do lose it indeed. For what is it else, when they hide it in the ground, taking it both from their own use and perchance from all other men's also? And yet thou, when thou hast hid thy treasure, as one out of all care hoppest for joy. The which treasure, if it should chance to be stolen, and thou ignorant of the theft shouldst die ten years after, all that ten years' space that thou livest after thy money was stolen, what matter was it to thee whether it had been taken away or else safe as thou leftest it? Truly both ways like profit came to thee.

To these so foolish pleasures they join dicers, whose madness they know by hearsay and not by use. Hunters also, and hawkers. For what pleasure is there (say they) in casting the dice upon a table, which thou hast done so often, that if there were any pleasure in it, yet the oft use might make thee weary thereof? Or what delight can there be, and not rather displeasure, in hearing the barking and howling of dogs? Or what greater pleasure is there to be felt when a dog followeth an hare than when a dog followeth a dog? For one thing is done in both, that is to say, running, if thou hast pleasure therein. But if the hope of slaughter and the expectation of tearing in pieces the beast doth please thee, thou shouldst rather be moved with pity to see a silly innocent hare murdered of a dog: the weak of the stronger, the fearful of the fierce, the innocent of the cruel and unmerciful. Therefore all this exercise of hunting, as a thing unworthy to be used of free men, the Utopians have rejected to their butchers, to the which craft (as we said before) they appoint their bondmen. For they count hunting the lowest, the vilest, and most abject part of butchery, and the other parts of it more profitable and more honest, as bringing much more commodity, in that they kill beasts only for necessity, whereas the hunter seeketh nothing but pleasure of the silly and woeful beast's slaughter and murder. The which pleasure in beholding death they think doth rise in the very beasts, either of a cruel affection of mind, or else to be changed in continuance of time into cruelty by long use of so cruel a pleasure.

These, therefore, and all suchlike, which be innumerable, though the common sort of people doth take them for pleasures, yet they, seeing there is no natural pleasantness in them, do plainly determine them to have no affinity with true and right pleasure. For as touching that they do commonly move the sense with delectation (which seemeth to be a work of pleasure), this doth nothing diminish their opinion. For not the nature of the thing, but their perverse and lewd custom is the cause hereof, which causeth them to accept bitter or sour things for sweet things even as women with child in their vitiate and corrupt taste think pitch and tallow sweeter than any honey. Howbeit, no man's judgment depraved and corrupt, either by sickness or by custom, can change the nature of pleasure more than it can do the nature of other things.

They make divers kinds of true pleasures. For some they attribute to the soul and some to the body. To the soul they give intelligence and that delectation that cometh of the contemplation of truth. Hereunto is joined the pleasant remembrance of the good life past. The pleasure of the body they divide into two parts. The first is when delectation is sensibly felt and perceived, which many times chanceth by the renewing and refreshing of those parts which our natural heat drieth up. This cometh by meat and drink, and sometimes whiles those things be expulsed and voided, whereof is in the body over-great abundance. This pleasure is felt when we do our natural easement, or when we be doing the act of generation, or when the itching of any part is eased with rubbing or scratching. Sometimes pleasure riseth exhibiting to any member nothing that it desireth, nor taking from it any pain that it feeleth, which nevertheless tickleth and moveth our senses with a certain secret efficacy, but with a manifest motion turneth them to it; as is that which cometh of music. The second part of bodily pleasure, they say, is that which consisteth and resteth in the quiet and upright state of the body. And that truly is every man's own proper health, intermingled and disturbed with no grief. For this, if it be not letted nor assaulted with no grief, is delectable of itself, though it be moved with no external or outward pleasure. For though it be not so plain and manifest to the sense as the greedy lust of eating and drinking, yet, nevertheless, many take it for the chiefest pleasure. All the Utopians grant it to be a right sovereign pleasure and, as you would say, the foundation and ground of all pleasures, as which even alone is able to make the state and condition of life delectable and pleasant; and it being once taken away, there is no place left for any pleasure. For to be without grief not having health, that they call insensibility and not pleasure.

The Utopians have long ago rejected and condemned the opinion of them which said that steadfast and quiet health (for this question also hath been diligently debated among them) ought not therefore to be counted a pleasure, because, they say, it cannot be presently and sensibly perceived and felt by some outward motion. But of the contrary part now they agree almost all in this, that health is a most sovereign pleasure. For seeing that in sickness (say they) is grief, which is a mortal enemy to pleasure, even as sickness is to health, why should not then pleasure be in the quietness of health? For they say it maketh nothing to this matter, whether you say that sickness is a grief, or that in sickness is grief, for all cometh to one purpose. For whether health be a pleasure itself, or a necessary cause of pleasure, as fire is of heat, truly both ways it followeth that they cannot be without pleasure that be in perfect health. Furthermore, whiles we eat (say they), then health, which began to be appaired, fighteth by the help of food against hunger. In the which fight, whiles health by little and little getteth the upper hand, that same proceeding and (as ye would say) that onwardness to the wont strength ministreth that pleasure whereby we be so refreshed. Health, therefore, which in the conflict is joyful, shall it not be merry when it hath gotten the victory? But as soon as it hath recovered the pristinate strength, which thing only in all the fight it coveted, shall it incontinent be astonied? Nor shall it not know nor embrace the own wealth and goodness? For where it is said health cannot be felt, this, they think, is nothing true. For what man waking, say they, feeleth not himself in health, but he that is not? Is there any man so possessed with stonish insensibility or with lethargy, that is to say, the sleeping sickness, that he will not grant health to be acceptable to him, and delectable?

But what other thing is delectation than that which by another name is called pleasure? They embrace chiefly the pleasures of the mind, for them they count the chiefest and most principal of all. The chief part of them they think doth come of the exercise of virtue and conscience of good life. Of these pleasures that the body ministreth, they give the pre-eminence to health. For the delight of eating and drinking, and whatsoever hath any like pleasantness, they determine to be pleasures much to be desired, but no other ways than for health's sake. For such things of their own proper nature be not so pleasant, but in that they resist sickness privily stealing on. Therefore, like as it is a wise man's part rather to avoid sickness than to wish for medicines, and rather to drive away and put to flight careful griefs than to call for comfort, so it is much better not to need this kind of pleasure than thereby to be eased of the contrary grief. The which kind of pleasure if any man take for his felicity, that man must needs grant that then he shall be in most felicity, if he live that life which is led in continual hunger, thirst, itching, eating, drinking, scratching, and rubbing. The which life how not only foul and unhonest, but also how miserable and wretched it is, who perceiveth not? These doubtless be the basest pleasures of all, as unpure and unperfect. For they never come, but accompanied with their contrary griefs, as with the pleasure of eating is joined hunger, and that after no very equal sort. For of these two the grief is both the more vehement and also of longer continuance, for it beginneth before the pleasure, and endeth not until the pleasure die with it.

Wherefore such pleasures they think not greatly to be set by, but in that they be necessary. Howbeit, they have delight also in these, and thankfully knowledge the tender love of mother nature, which with most pleasant delectation allureth her children to that, to the necessary use whereof they must from time to time continually be forced and driven. For how wretched and miserable should our life be, if these daily griefs of hunger and thirst could not be driven away but with bitter potions and sour medicines, as the other diseases be wherewith we be seldomer troubled? But beauty, strength, nimbleness, these as peculiar and pleasant gifts of nature they make much of. But those pleasures that be received by the ears, the eyes, and the nose, which nature willeth to be proper and peculiar to man (for no other living creature doth behold the fairness and the beauty of the world or is moved with any respect of savours, but only for the diversity of meats, neither perceiveth the concordant and discordant distances of sounds and tunes), these pleasures, I say, they accept and allow as certain pleasant rejoicings of life. But in all things this cautel they use, that a less pleasure hinder not a bigger, and that the pleasure be no cause of displeasure, which they think to follow of necessity if the pleasure be unhonest. But yet to despise the comeliness of beauty, to waste the bodily strength, to turn nimbleness into sluggishness, to consume and make feeble the body with fasting, to do injury to health, and to reject the pleasant motions of nature (unless a man neglect these commodities whiles he doth with a fervent zeal procure the wealth of others or the common profit, for the which pleasure forborne he is in hope of a greater pleasure at God's hand), else for a vain shadow of virtue for the wealth and profit of no man, to punish himself, or to the intent he may be able courageously to suffer adversity (which perchance shall never come to him), this to do they think it a point of extreme madness, and a token of a man cruelly minded towards himself and unkind towards nature, as one so disdaining to be in her danger, that he renounceth and refuseth all her benefits.

This is their sentence and opinion of virtue and pleasure, and they believe that by man's reason none can be found truer than this, unless any godlier be inspired into man from heaven. Wherein whether they believe well or no, neither the time doth suffer us to discuss, neither it is now necessary. For we have taken upon us to shew and declare their laws and ordinances, and not to defend them. But this thing I believe verily: howsoever these decrees be, that there is in no place of the world neither a more excellent people, neither a more flourishing commonwealth. They be light and quick of body, full of activity and nimbleness, and of more strength than a man would judge them by their stature, which for all that is not too low. And though their soil be not very fruitful, nor their air very wholesome, yet against the air they so defend them with temperate diet, and so order and husband their ground with diligent travail, that in no country is greater increase and plenty of corn and cattle, nor men's bodies of longer life and subject or apt to fewer diseases. There, therefore, a man may see well and diligently exploited and furnished, not only those things which husbandmen do commonly in other countries, as by craft and cunning to remedy the barrenness of the ground, but also a whole wood by the hands of the people plucked up by the roots in one place, and set again in another place. Wherein was had regard and consideration, not of plenty, but of commodious carriage, that wood and timber might be nigher to the sea or the rivers or the cities; for it is less labour and business to carry grain far by land than wood. The people be gentle, merry, quick, and fine witted, delighting in quietness and, when need requireth, able to abide and suffer much bodily labour. Else they be not greatly desirous and fond of it; but in the exercise and study of the mind they be never weary.

When they had heard me speak of the Greek literature or learning (for in Latin there was nothing that I thought they would greatly allow, besides historians and poets) they made wonderful earnest and importunate suit unto me that I would teach and instruct them in that tongue and learning. I began, therefore, to read unto them at the first, truly, more because I would not seem to refuse the labour than that I hoped that they would anything profit therein. But when I had gone forward a little, I perceived incontinent by their diligence that my labour should not be bestowed in vain. For they began so easily to fashion their letters, so plainly to pronounce the words, so quickly to learn by heart, and so surely to rehearse the same, that I marvelled at it, saving that the most part of them were fine and chosen wits, and of ripe age, picked out of the company of the learned men which not only of their own free and voluntary will, but also by the commandment of the council, undertook to learn this language. Therefore in less than three years' space there was nothing in the Greek tongue that they lacked. They were able to read good authors without any stay, if the book were not false. This kind of learning, as I suppose, they took so much the sooner because, it is somewhat alliant to them. For I think that this nation took their beginning of the Greeks, because their speech, which in all other points is not much unlike the Persian tongue, keepeth divers signs and tokens of the Greek language in the names of their cities and of their magistrates.

They have of me (for when I was determined to enter into my fourth voyage, I cast into the ship in the stead of merchandise a pretty fardel of books, because I intended to come again rather never than shortly), they have, I say, of me the most part of Plato's works, more of Aristotle's, also Theophrastus of plants, but in divers places (which I am sorry for) unperfect. For whiles we were a-shipboard a marmoset chanced upon the book as it was negligently laid by, which wantonly playing therewith plucked out certain leaves and tore them in pieces. Of them that have written the grammar, they have only Lascaris, for Theodorus I carried not with me, nor never a dictionary but Hesychius and Dioscorides. They set great store by Plutarch's books, and they be delighted with Lucian's merry conceits and jests. Of the poets they have Aristophanes, Homer, Euripides, and Sophocles in Aldus' small print. Of the historians they have Thucydides, Herodotus, and Herodian. Also, my companion Tricius Apinatus carried with him physic books, certain small works of Hippocrates, and Galen's *Microtechne*. The which book they have in great estimation; for though there be almost no nation under heaven that hath less need of physic than they, yet this notwithstanding, physic is nowhere in greater honour, because they count the knowledge of it among the goodliest and most profitable parts of philosophy. For whiles they by the help of this philosophy search out the secret mysteries of nature, they think themselves to receive thereby not only wonderful great pleasure, but also to obtain great thanks and favour of the Author and Maker thereof. Whom they think, according to the fashion of other artificers, to have set forth the marvellous and gorgeous frame of the world for man with great affection intentively to behold. Whom only He hath made of wit and capacity to consider and understand the excellency of so great a work. And therefore He beareth (say they) more goodwill and love to the curious and diligent beholder and viewer of His work and marveller at the same than He doth to him which, like a very brute beast without wit and reason, or as one without sense or moving, hath no regard to so great and so wonderful a spectacle. The wits, therefore, of the Utopians, inured and exercised in learning, be marvellous quick in the invention of feats helping anything to the advantage and wealth of life. Howbeit, two feats they may thank us for, that is, the science of imprinting and the craft of making paper. And yet not only us, but chiefly and principally themselves.

For when we shewed to them Aldus his print in books of paper, and told them of the stuff whereof paper is made, and of the feat of graving letters, speaking somewhat more than we could plainly declare (for there was none of us that knew perfectly either the one or the other), they forthwith very wittily conjectured the thing. And whereas before they wrote only in skins, in barks of trees, and in reeds, now they have attempted to make paper and to imprint letters. And though at the first it proved not all of the best, yet by often assaying the same they shortly got the feat of both, and have so brought the matter about that if they had copies of Greek authors they could lack no books. But now they have no more than I rehearsed before, saving that by printing of books they have multiplied and increased the same into many thousands of copies. Whosoever cometh thither to see the land, being excellent in any gift of wit, or through much and long journeying well experienced and seen in the knowledge of many countries (for the which cause we were very welcome to them), him they receive and entertain wondrous gently and lovingly. For they have delight to hear what is done in every land, howbeit very few merchant men come thither. For what should they bring thither, unless it were iron, or else gold and silver, which they had rather carry home again? Also such things as are to be carried out of their land, they think it more wisdom to carry that gear forth themselves, than that other should come thither to fetch it, to the intent they may the better know the outlands on every side of them, and keep in use the feat and knowledge of sailing.

Of Bondmen, Sick Persons, Wedlock, and divers other Matters

They neither make bondmen of prisoners taken in battle, unless it be in battle that they fought themselves, nor of bondmen's children, nor, to be short, of any such as they can get out of foreign countries, though he were there a bondman, but either such as among themselves for heinous offences be punished with bondage, or else such as in the cities of other lands for great trespasses be condemned to death. And of this sort of bondmen they have most store.

For many of them they bring home, sometimes paying very little for them, yea, most commonly getting them for gramercy. These sorts of bondmen they keep not only in continual work and labour, but also in bonds. But their own men they handle hardest, whom they judge more desperate, and to have deserved greater punishment, because they being so godly brought up to virtue in so excellent a commonwealth, could not for all that be refrained from misdoing. Another kind of bondmen they have, when a vile drudge being a poor labourer in another country doth choose of his own free will to be a bondman among them. These they entreat and order honestly, and entertain almost as gently as their own free citizens, saving that they put them to a little more labour, as thereto accustomed. If any such be disposed to depart thence (which seldom is seen) they neither hold him against his will, neither send him away with empty hands.

The sick (as I said) they see to with great affection, and let nothing at all pass concerning either physic or good diet, whereby they may be restored again to their health. Such as be sick of incurable diseases they comfort with sitting by them, with talking with them, and, to be short, with all manner of helps that may be. But if the disease be not only incurable, but also full of continual pain and anguish, then the priests and the magistrates exhort the man (seeing he is not able to do any duty of life, and by overliving his own death is noisome and irksome to other and grievous to himself), that he will determine with himself no longer to cherish that pestilent and painful disease; and, seeing his life is to him but a torment, that he will not be unwilling to die, but rather take a good hope to him, and either dispatch himself out of that painful life, as out of a prison or a rack of torment, or else suffer himself willingly to be rid out of it by other. And in so doing they tell him he shall do wisely, seeing by his death he shall lose no commodity, but end his pain. And because in that act he shall follow the counsel of the priests, that is to say, of the interpreters of God's will and pleasure, they shew him that he shall do like a godly and a virtuous man. They that be thus persuaded finish their lives willingly, either with hunger, or else die in their sleep without any feeling of death. But they cause none such to die against his will, nor they use no less diligence and attendance about him, believing this to be an honourable death. Else he that killeth himself before that the priests and the council have allowed the cause of his death, him as unworthy either to be buried or with fire to be consumed, they cast unburied into some stinking marsh.

The woman is not married before she be eighteen years old. The man is four years older before he marry. If either the man or the woman be proved to have actually offended, before their marriage, with another, the party that so hath trespassed is sharply punished, and both the offenders be forbidden ever after in all their life to marry, unless the fault be forgiven by the prince's pardon. But both the goodman and the goodwife of the house where that offence was committed, as being slack and negligent in looking to their charge, be in danger of great reproach and infamy. That offence is so sharply punished because they perceive that unless they be diligently kept from the liberty of this vice, few will join together in the love of marriage, wherein all the life must be led with one, and also all the griefs and displeasures coming therewith patiently be taken and borne.

Furthermore, in choosing wives and husbands they observe earnestly and straitly a custom which seemed to us very fond and foolish. For a sad and an honest matron sheweth the woman, be she maid or widow, naked to the wooer. And likewise a sage and discreet man exhibiteth the wooer naked to the woman. At this custom we laughed, and disallowed it as foolish. But they, on the other part, do greatly wonder at the folly of all other nations which, in buying a colt, whereas a little money is in hazard, be so chary and circumspect, that though he be almost all bare, yet they will not buy him unless the saddle and all the harness be taken off, lest under those coverings be hid some gall or sore. And yet in choosing a wife, which shall be either pleasure or displeasure to them all their life after, they be so reckless, that all the residue of the woman's body being covered with clothes, they esteem her scarcely by one handbreadth (for they can see no more but her face), and so to join her to them not without great jeopardy of evil agreeing together, if anything in her body afterward should chance to offend and mislike them. For all men be not so wise as to have respect to the virtuous conditions of the party. And the endowments of the body cause the virtues of the mind more to be esteemed and regarded, yea, even in the marriages of wise men. Verily so foul deformity may be hid under those coverings, that it may quite alienate and take away the man's mind from his wife, when it shall not be lawful for their bodies to be separate again. If such deformity happen by any chance after the marriage is consummate and finished, well, there is no remedy but patience. Every man must take his fortune well a worth. But it were well done that a law were made whereby all such deceits might be eschewed and avoided beforehand.

And this were they constrained more earnestly to look upon, because they only of the nations in that part of the world be content every man with one wife apiece. And matrimony is there never broken but by death, except adultery break the bond, or else the intolerable wayward manners of either party. For if either of them find themself for any such cause grieved, they may by the licence of the council change and take another. But the other party liveth ever after in infamy and out of wedlock. Howbeit, the husband to put away his wife for no other fault but for that some mishap is fallen to her body, this by no means they will suffer. For they judge it a great point of cruelty that anybody in their most need of help and comfort should be cast off and forsaken, and that old age, which both bringeth sickness with it and is a sickness itself, should unkindly and unfaithfully be dealt withal. But now and then it chanceth whereas the man and the woman cannot well agree between themselves, both of them finding other, with whom they hope to live more quietly and merrily, that they by the full consent of them both be divorced asunder and married again to other. But that not without the authority of the council, which agreeth to no divorces before they and their wives have diligently tried and examined the matter. Yea, and then also they be loath to consent to it, because they know this to be the next way to break love between man and wife, to be in easy hope of a new marriage.

Breakers of wedlock be punished with most grievous bondage; and if both the offenders were married, then the parties which in that behalf have suffered wrong, being divorced from the avoutrers, be married together, if they will, or else to whom they lust. But if either of them both do still continue in love toward so unkind a bedfellow, the use of wedlock is not to them forbidden, if the party faultless be disposed to follow in toiling and drudgery the person which for that offence is condemned to bondage. And very oft it chanceth that the repentance of the one and the earnest diligence of the other doth so move the prince with pity and compassion, that he restoreth the bond person from servitude to liberty and freedom again. But if the same party be taken eftsoons in that fault, there is no other way but death. To other trespasses no prescript punishment is appointed by any law; but according to the heinousness of the offence, or contrary, so the punishment is moderated by the discretion of the council. The husbands chastise their wives, and the parents their children, unless they have done any so horrible an offence, that the open punishment thereof maketh much for the advancement of honest manners.

But most commonly the most heinous faults be punished with the incommodity of bondage. For that they suppose to be to the offenders no less grief, and to the common-wealth more profit, than if they should hastily put them to death, and so make them quite out of the way. For there cometh more profit of their labour than of their death, and by their example they fear other the longer from like offences. But if they, being thus used, do rebel and kick again, then forsooth they be slain as desperate and wild beasts, whom neither prison nor chain could restrain and keep under. But they which take their bond-age patiently be not left all hopeless. For after they have been broken and tamed with long miseries, if then they shew such repentance as thereby it may be perceived that they be sorrier for their offence than for their punishment, sometimes by the prince's prerogative, and sometimes by the voice and consent of the people, their bondage either is mitigated or else clean released and forgiven. He that moveth to advoutry is in no less danger and jeopardy than if he had committed advoutry in deed. For in all offences they count the intent and pretenced purpose as evil as the act or deed itself, thinking that no let ought to excuse him that did his best to have no let.

They have singular delight and pleasure in fools. And as it is a great reproach to do any of them hurt or injury, so they prohibit not to take pleasure of foolishness. For that, they think, doth much good to the fools. And if any man be so sad and stern that he cannot laugh neither at their words nor at their deeds, none of them be committed to his tuition, for fear lest he would not entreat them gently and favourably enough: to whom they should bring no delectation (for other goodness in them is none), much less any profit should they yield him. To mock a man for his deformity or for that he lacketh any part or limb of his body is counted great dishonesty and reproach, not to him that is mocked, but to him that mocketh, which unwisely doth embraid any man of that as a vice that was not in his power to eschew.

Also, as they count and reckon very little wit to be in him that regardeth not natural beauty and comeliness, so to help the same with paintings is taken for a vain and a wanton pride, not without great infamy. For they know, even by very experience, that no comeliness of beauty doth so highly commend and advance the wives in the conceit of their husbands as honest conditions and lowliness. For as love is oftentimes won with beauty, so it is not kept, preserved and continued but by virtue and obedience. They do not only fear their people from doing evil by punishments, but also allure them to virtue with rewards of honour. Therefore they set up in the marketplace the images of notable men and of such as have been great and bountiful benefactors to the commonwealth, for the perpetual memory of their good acts, and also that the glory and renown of the ancestors may stir and provoke their posterity to virtue. He that inordinately and ambitiously desireth promotions is left all hopeless for ever attaining any promotion as long as he liveth.

They live together lovingly, for no magistrate is either haughty or fearful. Fathers they be called, and like fathers they use themselves. The citizens (as it is their duty) willingly exhibit unto them due honour without any compulsion. Nor the prince himself is not known from the other by princely apparel or a robe of state, nor by a crown or diadem royal or cap of maintenance, but by a little sheaf of corn carried before him. And so a taper of wax is borne before the bishop, whereby only he is known.

They have but few laws, for to people so instruct and institute very few do suffice. Yea, this thing they chiefly reprove among other nations, that innumerable books of laws and expositions upon the same be not sufficient. But they think it against all right and justice that men should be bound to those laws which either be in number more than be able to be read, or else blinder and darker than that any man can well understand them. Furthermore, they utterly exclude and banish all attorneys, proctors, and sergeants at the law, which craftily handle matters, and subtly dispute of the laws. For they think it most meet that every man should plead his own matter, and tell the same tale before the judge that he would tell to his man of law. So shall there be less circumstance of words, and the truth shall sooner come to light, whiles the judge with a discreet judgment doth weigh the words of him whom no lawyer hath instruct with deceit, and whiles he helpeth and beareth out simple wits against the false and malicious circumventions of crafty children. This is hard to be observed in other countries, in so infinite a number of blind and intricate laws. But in Utopia every man is a cunning lawyer; for (as I said) they have very few laws, and the plainer and grosser that any interpretation is, that they allow as most just. For all laws (say they) be made and published only to the intent that by them every man should be put in remembrance of his duty. But the crafty and subtle interpretation of them (forasmuch as few can attain thereto) can put very few in that remembrance, whereas the simple, the plain, and gross meaning of the laws is open to every man. Else as touching the vulgar sort of the people, which be both most in number and have most need to know their duties, were it not as good for them that no law were made at all, as, when it is made, to bring so blind an interpretation upon it, that without great wit and long arguing no man can discuss it? To the finding out whereof neither the gross judgment of the people can attain, neither the whole life of them that be occupied in working for their livings can suffice thereto.

These virtues of the Utopians have caused their next neighbours and borderers, which live free and under no subjection (for the Utopians long ago have delivered many of them from tyranny), to take magistrates of them, some for a year and some for five years' space. Which, when the time of their office is expired, they bring home again with honour and praise, and take new again with them into their country. These nations have undoubtedly very well and wholesomely provided for their commonwealths. For seeing that both the making and marring of the weal-public doth depend and hang upon the manners of the rulers and magistrates, what officers could they more wisely have chosen than those which cannot be led from honesty by bribes (for to them that shortly after shall depart thence into their own country money should be unprofitable) nor yet be moved either with favour or malice towards any man, as being strangers and unacquainted with the people? The which two vices of affection and avarice, where they take place in judgments, incontinent they break justice, the strongest and surest bond of a commonwealth. These peoples which fetch their officers and rulers from them, the Utopians call their fellows. And others to whom they have been beneficial, they call their friends.

As touching leagues, which in other places between country and country be so oft concluded, broken, and renewed, they never make none with any nation. For to what purpose serve leagues, say they, as though nature had not set sufficient love between man and man? And who so regardeth not nature, think you that he will pass for words? They be brought into this opinion chiefly because that in those parts of the world leagues between princes be wont to be kept and observed very slenderly. For here in Europe, and especially in these parts where the faith and religion of Christ reigneth, the majesty of leagues is everywhere esteemed holy and inviolable, partly through the justice and goodness of princes, and partly at the reverence and motion of the head bishops. Which, like as they make no promise themselves but they do very religiously perform the same, so they exhort all princes in any wise to abide by their promises, and them that refuse or deny so to do, by their pontifical power and authority they compel thereto. And surely they think well that it might seem a very reproachful thing if, in the leagues of them which by a peculiar name be called faithful, faith should have no place. But in that new found part of the world, which is scarcely so far from us beyond the line equinoctial as our life and manners be dissident from theirs, no trust nor confidence is in leagues. But the more and holier ceremonies the league is knit up with, the sooner it is broken by some cavillation found in the words, which many times of purpose be so craftily put in and placed, that the bands can never be so sure nor so strong but they will find some hole open to creep out at, and to break both league and truth. The which crafty dealing, yea, the which fraud and deceit, if they should know it to be practised among private men in their bargains and contracts, they would incontinent cry out at it with an open mouth and a sour countenance, as an offence most detestable, and worthy to be punished with a shameful death, yea, even they that advance themselves authors of like counsel given to princes. Wherefore it may well be thought, either that all justice is but a base and a low virtue and which avaleth itself far under the high dignity of kings, or, at the least wise, that there be two justices: the one meet for the inferior sort of the people, going afoot and creeping low by the ground, and bound down on every side with many bands because it shall not run at rovers; the other a princely virtue, which like as it is of much higher majesty than the other poor justice, so also it is of much more liberty, as to the which nothing is unlawful that it lusteth after. These manners of princes (as I said) which be there so evil keepers of leagues, cause the Utopians, as I suppose, to make no leagues at all, which perchance would change their mind if they lived here. Howbeit, they think that though leagues be never so faithfully observed and kept, yet the custom of making leagues was very evil begun. For this causeth men (as though nations which be separate asunder by the space of a little hill or a river were coupled together by no society or bond of nature) to think themselves born adversaries and enemies one to another, and that it were lawful for the one to seek the death and destruction of the other if leagues were not; yea, and that after the leagues be accorded, friendship doth not grow and increase, but the licence of robbing and stealing doth still remain, as far forth as, for lack of foresight and advisement in writing the words of the league, any sentence or clause to the contrary is not therein sufficiently comprehended. But they be of a contrary opinion, that is, that no man ought to be counted an enemy which hath done no injury; and that the fellowship of nature is a strong league, and that men be better and more surely knit together by love and benevolence than by covenants of leagues, by hearty affection of mind than by words.

Of Warfare

War or battle as a thing very beastly, and yet to no kind of beasts in so much use as to man, they do detest and abhor. And, contrary to the custom almost of all other nations, they count nothing so much against glory as glory gotten in war. And therefore, though they do daily practise and exercise themselves in the discipline of war, and not only the men, but also the women upon certain appointed days, lest they should be to seek in the feat of arms if need should require, yet they never go to battle but either in the defence of their own country or to drive out of their friends' land the enemies that have invaded it, or by their power to deliver from the yoke and bondage of tyranny some people that be therewith oppressed. Which thing they do of mere pity and compassion. Howbeit, they send help to their friends, not ever in their defence, but sometimes also to requite and revenge injuries before to them done. But this they do not unless their counsel and advice in the matter be asked, whiles it is yet new and fresh. For if they find the cause probable, and if the contrary part will not restore again such things as be of them justly demanded, then they be the chief authors and makers of the war. Which they do not only as oft as by inroads and invasions of soldiers preys and booties be driven away, but then also much more mortally when their friends' merchants in any land, either under the pretence of unjust laws or else by the wresting and wrong understanding of good laws, do sustain an unjust accusation under the colour of justice.

Neither the battle which the Utopians fought for the Nephelogetes against the Alaopolitans a little before our time was made for any other cause, but that the Nephelogete merchantmen, as the Utopians thought, suffered wrong of the Alaopolitans under the pretence of right. But whether it were right or wrong, it was with so cruel and mortal war revenged, the countries round about joining their help and power to the puissance and malice of both parties, that most flourishing and wealthy peoples being some of them shrewdly shaken, and some of them sharply beaten, the mischiefs were not finished nor ended until the Alaopolitans at the last were yielded up as bondmen into the jurisdiction of the Nephelogetes. For the Utopians fought not this war for themselves. And yet the Nephelogetes before the war, when the Alaopolitans flourished in wealth, were nothing to be compared with them.

So eagerly the Utopians prosecute the injuries done to their friends: yea, in money matters, and not their own likewise. For if they by covin or guile be wiped beside their goods, so that no violence be done to their bodies, they wreak their anger by abstaining from occupying with that nation until they have made satisfaction. Not for because they set less store by their own citizens than by their friends, but that they take the loss of their friends' money more heavily than the loss of their own. Because that their friends' merchantmen, forasmuch as that they lose is their own private goods, sustain great damage by the loss. But their own citizens lose nothing but of the common goods, and of that which was at home plentiful and almost superfluous, else had it not been sent forth. Therefore no man feeleth the loss. And for this cause they think it too cruel an act to revenge that loss with the death of many, the incommodity of the which loss no man feeleth neither in his life nor yet in his living. But if it chance that any of their men in any other country be maimed or killed, whether it be done by a common or a private counsel, knowing and trying out the truth of the matter by their ambassadors, unless the offenders be rendered unto them in recompense of the injury, they will not be appeased, but incontinent they proclaim war against them. The offenders yielded, they punish either with death or with bondage. They be not only sorry, but also ashamed to achieve the victory with bloodshed, counting it great folly to buy precious wares too dear.

They rejoice and avaunt themselves, if they vanquish and oppress their enemies by craft and deceit. And for that act they make a general triumph, and as if the matter were manfully handled, they set up a pillar of stone in the place where they so vanquished their enemies, in token of the victory. For then they glory, then they boast, and crack that they have played the men indeed when they have so overcome, as no other living creature but only man could: that is to say, by the might and puissance of wit. For with bodily strength (say they) bears, lions, boars, wolves, dogs, and other wild beasts do fight. And as the most part of them do pass us in strength and fierce courage, so in wit and reason we be much stronger than they all.

Their chief and principal purpose in war is to obtain that thing, which if they had before obtained, they would not have moved battle. But if that be not possible, they take so cruel vengeance of them which be in the fault, that ever after they be afeard to do the like. This is their chief and principal intent, which they immediately and first of all prosecute and set forward, but yet so that they be more circumspect in avoiding and eschewing jeopardies than they be desirous of praise and renown. Therefore immediately after that war is once solemnly denounced, they procure many proclamations signed with their own common seal to be set up privily at one time in their enemy's land in places most frequented. In these proclamations they promise great rewards to him that will kill their enemy's prince, and somewhat less gifts, but them very great also, for every head of them whose names be in the said proclamations contained. They be those whom they count their chief adversaries, next unto the prince. Whatsoever is prescribed unto him that killeth any of the proclaimed persons, that is doubled to him that bringeth any of the same to them alive; yea, and to the proclaimed persons themselves, if they will change their minds and come in to them, taking their parts, they proffer the same great rewards with pardon and surety of their lives. Therefore it quickly cometh to pass that their enemies have all other men in suspicion, and be unfaithful and mistrusting among themselves one to another, living in great fear and in no less jeopardy. For it is well known, that divers times the most part of them (and specially the prince himself) hath been betrayed of them in whom they put their most hope and trust. So that there is no manner of act nor deed that gifts and rewards do not enforce men unto. And in rewards they keep no measure, but, remembering and considering into how great hazard and jeopardy they call them, endeavour themselves to recompense the greatness of the danger with like great benefits. And therefore they promise not only wonderful great abundance of gold, but also lands of great revenues lying in most safe places among their friends. And their promises they perform faithfully without any fraud or covin.

This custom of buying and selling adversaries among other people is disallowed as a cruel act of a base and a cowardly mind. But they in this behalf think themselves much praiseworthy, as who like wise men by this means dispatch great wars without any battle or skirmish. Yea, they count it also a deed of pity and mercy, because that by the death of a few offenders the lives of a great number of innocents, as well of their own men as also of their enemies, be ransomed and saved, which in fighting should have been slain. For they do no less pity the base and common sort of their enemies' people, than they do their own, knowing that they be driven and enforced to war against their wills by the furious madness of their princes and heads. If by none of these means the matter go forward as they would have it, then they procure occasions of debate, and dissension to be spread among their enemies, as by bringing the prince's brother or some of the noblemen in hope to obtain the kingdom. If this way prevail not, then they raise up the people that be next neighbours and borderers to their enemies, and them they set in their necks under the colour of some old title of right, such as kings do never lack. To them they promise their help and aid in their war; and as for money, they give them abundance. But of their own citizens they send to them few or none, whom they make so much of and love so entirely, that they would not be willing to change any of them for their adversaries' prince. But their gold and silver, because they keep it all for this only purpose, they lay it out frankly and freely, as who should live even as wealthily if they had bestowed it every penny.

Yea, and besides their riches which they keep at home, they have also an infinite treasure abroad, by reason that (as I said before) many nations be in their debt. Therefore they hire soldiers out of all countries and send them to battle, but chiefly of the Zapoletes. This people is 500 miles from Utopia eastward. They be hideous, savage, and fierce, dwelling in wild woods and high mountains where they were bred and brought up. They be of an hard nature, able to abide and sustain heat, cold, and labour, abhorring from all delicate dainties, occupying no husbandry nor tillage of the ground, homely and rude both in building of their houses and in their apparel, given unto no goodness, but only to the breeding and bringing up of cattle. The most part of their living is by hunting and stealing. They be born only to war, which they diligently and earnestly seek for, and when they have gotten it they be wondrous glad thereof. They go forth of their country in great companies together, and whosoever lacketh soldiers, there they proffer their service for small wages. This is only the craft they have to get their living by. They maintain their life by seeking their death. For them whomwith they be in wages they fight hardly, fiercely, and faithfully. But they bind themselves for no certain time; but upon this condition they enter into bonds, that the next day they will take part with the other side for greater wages, and the next day after that they will be ready to come back again for a little more money. There be few wars thereaway, wherein is not a great number of them in both parties. Therefore it daily chanceth that nigh kinsfolk which were hired together on one part, and there very friendly and familiarly used themselves one with another, shortly after being separate in contrary parts, run one against another enviously and fiercely, and, forgetting both kindred and friendship, thrust their swords one in another. And that for none other cause but that they be hired of contrary princes for a little money, which they do so highly regard and esteem, that they will easily be provoked to change parts for a halfpenny more wages by the day, so quickly they have taken a smack in covetousness, which for all that is to them no profit. For that they get by fighting, immediately they spend unthriftily and wretchedly in riot.

This people fighteth for the Utopians against all nations, because they give them greater wages than any other nation will. For the Utopians, like as they seek good men to use well, so they seek these evil and vicious men to abuse, whom, when need requireth, with promises of great rewards they put forth into great jeopardies. From whence the most part of them never cometh again to ask their rewards. But to them that remain alive they pay that which they promised faithfully, that they may be the more willing to put themselves in like danger another time. Nor the Utopians pass not how many of them they bring to destruction, for they believe that they should do a very good deed for all mankind if they could rid out of the world all that foul stinking den of that most wicked and cursed people. Next unto this they use the soldiers of them for whom they fight, and then the help of their other friends, and last of all they join to their own citizens, among whom they give to one of tried virtue and prowess the rule, governance, and conduction of the whole army. Under him they appoint two other which, whiles he is safe, be both private and out of office. But if he be taken or slain, the one of the other two succeedeth him, as it were by inheritance. And if the second miscarry, then the third taketh his room, lest that (as the chance of battle is uncertain and doubtful) the jeopardy or death of the captain should bring the whole army in hazard. They choose soldiers out of every city those which put forth themselves willingly, for they thrust no man forth into war against his will, because they believe if any man be fearful and faint-hearted of nature he will not only do no manful and hardy act himself, but also be occasion of cowardness to his fellows. But if any battle be made against their own country, then they put these cowards (so that they be strong-bodied) in ships among other bold-hearted men. Or else they dispose them upon the walls, from whence they may not fly. Thus what for shame that their enemies be at hand, and what for because they be without hope of running away, they forget all fear. And many times extreme necessity turneth cowardness into prowess and manliness.

But as none of them is thrust forth of his country into war against his will, so women that be willing to accompany their husbands in times of war be not prohibited or letted. Yea, they provoke and exhort them to it with praises, and in set field the wives do stand every one by their own husband's side. Also every man is compassed next about with his own children, kinsfolk, and alliance, that they whom nature chiefly moveth to mutual succour, thus standing together, may help one another. It is a great reproach and dishonesty for the husband to come home without his wife, or the wife without her husband, or the son without his father. And therefore if the other part stick so hard by it that the battle come to their hands, it is fought with great slaughter and bloodshed, even to the utter destruction of both parts. For as they make all the means and shifts that may be to keep themselves from the necessity of fighting or that they may dispatch the battle by their hired soldiers, so when there is no remedy, but that they must needs fight themselves, then they do as courageously fall to it, as before, whiles they might, they did wisely avoid and refuse it. Nor they be not most fierce at the first brunt. But in continuance by little and little their fierce courage increaseth with so stubborn and obstinate minds, that they will rather die than give back an inch. For that surety of living which every man hath at home being joined with no careful anxiety or remembrance how their posterity shall live after them (for this pensiveness oftentimes breaketh and abateth courageous stomachs) maketh them stout and hardy and disdainful to be conquered. Moreover, their knowledge in chivalry and feats of arms putteth them in a good hope. Finally the wholesome and virtuous opinions wherein they were brought up even from their childhood, partly through learning and partly through the good ordinances and laws of their weal-public, augment and increase their manful courage. By reason whereof they neither set so little store by their lives that they will rashly and unadvisedly cast them away, nor they be not so far in lewd and fond love therewith, that they will shamefully covet to keep them when honesty biddeth leave them.

When the battle is hottest and in all places most fierce and fervent, a band of chosen and picked young men, which be sworn to live and die together, take upon them to destroy their adversaries' captain, whom they invade, now with privy wiles, now by open strength. At him they strike both near and far off. He is assailed with a long and a continual assault, fresh men still coming in the wearied men's places. And seldom it chanceth (unless he save himself by flying) that he is not either slain, or else taken prisoner and yielded to his enemies alive. If they win the field they persecute not their enemies with the violent rage of slaughter, for they had rather take them alive than

kill them. Neither they do so follow the chase and pursuit
of their enemies, but they leave behind them one part of
their host in battle array under their standards. Insomuch
that if all their whole army be discomfited and overcome,
saving the rearward, and that they therewith achieve the
victory, then they had rather let all their enemies escape
than to follow them out of array. For they remember it
hath chanced unto themselves more than once, the whole
power and strength of their host being vanquished and
put to flight whiles their enemies rejoicing in the victory
have persecuted them flying some one way and some
another, a small company of their men lying in an ambush,
there ready at all occasions, have suddenly risen upon
them thus dispersed and scattered out of array and
through presumption of safety unadvisedly pursuing the
chase, and have incontinent changed the fortune of the
whole battle, and spite of their teeth wresting out of their
hands the sure and undoubted victory, being a little
before conquered, have for their part conquered the con-
querors. It is hard to say whether they be craftier in laying
an ambush, or wittier in avoiding the same. You would
think they intend to fly when they mean nothing less;
and contrariwise, when they go about that purpose you
would believe it were the least part of their thought.
For if they perceive themselves either overmatched in
number or closed in too narrow a place, then they remove
their camp; either in the night season with silence or by
some policy they deceive their enemies, or in the daytime
they retire back so softly, that it is no less jeopardy to
meddle with them when they give back than when they
press on.

They fence and fortify their camp surely with a deep
and a broad trench. The earth thereof is cast inward. Nor
they do not set drudges and slaves awork about it; it is
done by the hands of the soldiers themselves. All the
whole army worketh upon it, except them that keep
watch and ward in harness before the trench for sudden
adventures. Therefore, by the labour of so many a large

trench closing in a great compass of ground is made in less time than any man would believe. Their armour or harness which they wear is sure and strong to receive strokes, and handsome for all movings and gestures of the body, insomuch that it is not unwieldy to swim in. For in the discipline of their warfare among other feats they learn to swim in harness. Their weapons be arrows aloof, which they shoot both strongly and surely, not only foot-men, but also horsemen. At hand strokes they use not swords but pole-axes, which be mortal as well in sharpness as in weight, both for foins and downstrokes. Engines for war they devise and invent wondrous wittily. Which when they be made they keep very secret, lest, if they should be known before need require, they should be but laughed at and serve to no purpose. But in making them, hereunto they have chief respect, that they be both easy to be carried and handsome to be moved and turned about. Truce taken with their enemies for a short time they do so firmly and faithfully keep, that they will not break it, no, not though they be thereunto provoked. They do not waste nor destroy their enemies' land with foragings, nor they burn not up their corn. Yea, they save it as much as may be from being overrun and trodden down either with men or horses, thinking that it groweth for their own use and profit. They hurt no man that is unarmed, unless he be an espial.

All cities that be yielded unto them they defend; and such as they win by force of assault they neither despoil nor sack, but them that withstood and dissuaded the yielding up of the same they put to death. The other soldiers they punish with bondage. All the weak multi-tude they leave untouched. If they know that any citizens counselled to yield and render up the city, to them they give part of the condemned men's goods. The residue they distribute and give freely among them whose help they had in the same war, for none of themselves taketh any portion of the prey. But when the battle is finished and ended, they put their friends to never a penny cost of all the charges that they were at, but lay it upon their necks that be conquered. Them they burden with the whole charge of their expenses, which they demand of them partly in money to be kept for like use of battle, and partly in lands of great revenues to be paid unto them yearly for ever. Such revenues they have now in many countries. Which, by little and little rising of divers and sundry causes, be increased above seven hundred thousand ducats by the year. Thither they send forth some of their citizens as lieutenants, to live there sumptuously like men of honour and renown. And yet, this notwithstanding, much money is saved which cometh to the common treasury, unless it so chance that they had rather trust the country with the money. Which many times they do so long until they have need to occupy it; and it seldom happeneth that they demand all. Of these lands they assign part unto them which at their request and exhortation put themselves in such jeopardies as I spake of before. If any prince stir up war against them, intending to invade their land, they meet him incontinent out of their own borders with great power and strength. For they never lightly make war in their own country, nor they be never brought into so extreme necessity as to take help out of foreign lands into their own island.

Of the Religions in Utopia

There be divers kinds of religion not only in sundry parts of the island, but also in divers places of every city. Some worship for god the sun, some the moon, some some other of the planets. There be that give worship to a man that was once of excellent virtue or of famous glory, not only as god, but also as the chiefest and highest god. But the most and the wisest part, rejecting all these, believe that there is a certain godly power unknown, everlasting, incomprehensible, inexplicable, far above the capacity and reach of man's wit, dispersed throughout all the world, not in bigness, but in virtue and power. Him they call the father of all. To him alone they attribute the beginnings, the increasings, the proceedings, the changes, and the ends of all things. Neither they give any divine honours to any other than to him. Yea, all the other also, though they be in divers opinions, yet in this point they agree all together with the wisest sort in believing that there is one chief and principal god, the maker and ruler of the whole world, whom they all commonly in their country language call Mithra. But in this they disagree, that among some he is counted one, and among some another. For every one of them, whatsoever that is which he taketh for the chief god, thinketh it to be the very same nature to whose only divine might and majesty the sum and sovereignty of all things by the consent of all people is attributed and given. Howbeit, they all begin by little and little to forsake and fall from this variety of superstitions, and to agree together in that religion which seemeth by reason to pass and excel the residue. And it is not to be doubted but all the other would long ago have been abolished, but that whatsoever unprosperous thing happened to any of them, as he was minded to change his religion, the fearfulness of people did take it, not as a thing coming by chance, but as sent from God out of heaven, as though the god whose honour he was forsaking would revenge that wicked purpose against him.

But after they heard us speak of the name of Christ, of His doctrine, laws, miracles, and of the no less wonderful constancy of so many martyrs, whose blood willingly shed brought a great number of nations throughout all parts of the world into their sect, you will not believe with how glad minds they agreed unto the same, whether it were by the secret inspiration of God, or else for that they thought it nighest unto that opinion which among them is counted the chiefest. Howbeit, I think this was no small help and furtherance in the matter, that they heard us say that Christ instituted among His all things common, and that the same community doth yet remain amongst the rightest Christian companies. Verily, howsoever it came to pass, many of them consented together in our religion and were washed in the holy water of baptism. But because among us four (for no more of us was left alive, two of our company being dead) there was no priest, which I am right sorry for, they being entered and instructed in all other points of our religion, lack only those sacraments which here none but priests do minister. Howbeit, they understand and perceive them and be very desirous of the same. Yea, they reason and dispute the matter earnestly among themselves, whether, without the sending of a Christian bishop, one chosen out of their own people may receive the order of priesthood. And truly they were minded to choose one, but at my departure from them they had chosen none.

They also which do not agree to Christ's religion fear no man from it nor speak against any man that hath received it, saving that one of our company in my presence was sharply punished. He, as soon as he was baptized, began against our wills, with more earnest affection than wisdom, to reason of Christ's religion, and began to wax so hot in his matter, that he did not only prefer our religion before all other, but also did utterly despise and condemn all other, calling them profane, and the followers of them wicked and devilish and the children of everlasting damnation. When he had thus long reasoned the matter they laid hold on him, accused him, and condemned him into exile, not as a despiser of religion but as a seditious person and a raiser up of dissension among the people. For this is one of the ancientest laws among them, that no man shall be blamed for reasoning in the maintenance of his own religion. For King Utopus, even at the first beginning hearing that the inhabitants of the land were before his coming thither at continual dissension and strife among themselves for their religions, perceiving also that this common dissension (whiles every several sect took several parts in fighting for their country) was the only occasion of his conquest over them all, as soon as he had gotten the victory, first of all he made a decree that it should be lawful for every man to favour and follow what religion he would, and that he might do the best he could to bring other to his opinion, so that he did it peaceably, gently, quietly, and soberly, without hasty and contentious rebuking and inveighing against others. If he could not by fair and gentle speech induce them unto his opinion, yet he should use no kind of violence, and refrain from displeasant and seditious words. To him that would vehemently and fervently in this cause strive and contend was decreed banishment or bondage.

This law did King Utopus make, not only for the maintenance of peace, which he saw through continual contention and mortal hatred utterly extinguished, but also because he thought this decree should make for the furtherance of religion. Whereof he durst define and determine nothing unadvisedly, as doubting whether God, desiring manifold and diverse sorts of honour, would inspire sundry men with sundry kinds of religion. And this surely he thought a very unmeet and foolish thing, and a point of arrogant presumption, to compel all other by violence and threatenings to agree to the same that thou believest to be true. Furthermore, though there be one religion which alone is true, and all other vain and superstitious, yet did he well foresee (so that the matter were handled with reason and sober modesty) that the truth of its own power would at the last issue out and come to light. But if contention and debate in that behalf should continually be used, as the worst men be most obstinate and stubborn and in their evil opinion most constant, he perceived that then the best and holiest religion would be trodden underfoot and destroyed by most vain superstitions, even as good corn is by thorns and weeds overgrown and choked. Therefore all this matter he left undiscussed, and gave to every man free liberty and choice to believe what he would; saving that he earnestly and straitly charged them that no man should conceive so vile and base an opinion of the dignity of man's nature as to think that the souls do die and perish with the body, or that the world runneth at all aventures, governed by no divine providence.

And therefore they believe that after this life vices be extremely punished and virtues bountifully rewarded. Him that is of a contrary opinion they count not in the number of men, as one that hath avaled the high nature of his soul to the vileness of brute beasts' bodies, much less in the number of their citizens whose laws and ordinances, if it were not for fear, he would nothing at all esteem. For you may be sure that he will study either with craft privily to mock, or else violently to break, the common laws of his country, in whom remaineth no further fear than of the laws nor no further hope than of the body. Wherefore he that is thus minded is deprived of all honours, excluded from all offices, and reject from all common administrations in the weal-public. And thus he is of all sorts despised as of an unprofitable and of a base and vile nature. Howbeit, they put him to no punishment, because they be persuaded that it is in no man's power to believe what he list. No nor they constrain him not with threatenings to dissemble his mind and shew countenance contrary to his thought; for deceit and falsehood and all manners of lies, as next unto fraud, they do marvellously detest and abhor. But they suffer him not to dispute in his opinion, and that only among the common people. For else, apart among the priests and men of gravity they do not only suffer but also exhort him to dispute and argue, hoping that at the last that madness will give place to reason. There be also other, and of them no small number, which be not forbidden to speak their minds, as grounding their opinion upon some reason, being in their living neither evil nor vicious. Their heresy is much contrary to the other; for they believe that the souls of brute beasts be immortal and everlasting, but nothing to be compared with ours in dignity, neither ordained nor predestinate to like felicity. For all they believe certainly and surely that man's bliss shall be so great, that they do mourn and lament every man's sickness, but no man's

death, unless it be one whom they see depart from his
life carefully and against his will. For this they take for a
very evil token, as though the soul, being in despair and
vexed in conscience through some privy and secret
forefeeling of the punishment now at hand, were afeard
to depart. And they think he shall not be welcome to
God, which, when he is called, runneth not to Him gladly
but is drawn by force and sore against his will. They,
therefore, that see this kind of death do abhor it, and
them that so die they bury with sorrow and silence. And
when they have prayed God to be merciful to the soul
and mercifully to pardon the infirmities thereof, they
cover the dead corpse with earth. Contrariwise, all that
depart merrily and full of good hope, for them no man
mourneth, but followeth the hearse with joyful singing,
commending the souls to God with great affection. And
at the last, not with mourning sorrow, but with a great
reverence, they burn the bodies; and in the same place
they set up a pillar of stone with the dead man's titles
therein graved. When they be come home they rehearse
his virtuous manners and his good deeds, but no part of
his life is so oft or gladly talked of as his merry death.
They think that this remembrance of the virtue and goodness of the dead doth vehemently provoke and enforce
the living to virtue, and that nothing can be more pleasant
and acceptable to the dead whom they suppose to be
present among them when they talk of them, though to
the dull and feeble eyesight of mortal men they be invis-
ible. For it were an inconvenient thing that the blessed
should not be at liberty to go whither they would and it
were a point of great unkindness in them to have utterly
cast away the desire of visiting and seeing their friends to
whom they were in their lifetime joined by mutual love
and amity. Which in good men after their death they
count to be rather increased than diminished. They
believe, therefore, that the dead be presently conversant
among the quick as beholders and witnesses of all their
words and deeds. Therefore they go more courageously

to their business, as having a trust and affiance in such overseers. And this same belief of the present conversation of their forefathers and ancestors among them feareth them from all secret dishonesty. They utterly despise and mock soothsayings and divinations of things to come by the flight or voices of birds, and all other divinations of vain superstition, which in other countries be in great observation. But they highly esteem and worship miracles that come by no help of nature, as works and witnesses of the present power of God; and such they say do chance there very often. And sometimes in great and doubtful matters by common intercession and prayers they procure and obtain them with a sure hope and confidence and a steadfast belief.

They think that the contemplation of nature and the praise thereof coming is to God a very acceptable honour. Yet there be many so earnestly bent and affectioned to religion, that they pass nothing for learning, nor give their minds to any knowledge of things. But idleness they utterly forsake and eschew, thinking felicity after this life to be gotten and obtained by busy labours and good exercises. Some, therefore, of them attend upon the sick, some amend highways, cleanse ditches, repair bridges, dig turfs, gravel, and stones, fell and cleave wood, bring wood, corn, and other things into the cities in carts, and serve not only in common works, but also in private labours as servants, yea, more than bondmen. For whatsoever unpleasant, hard, and vile work is anywhere from the which labour, loathsomeness, and desperation doth fray other, all that they take upon them willingly and gladly, procuring quiet and rest to other, remaining in continual work and labour themselves, not embraiding others therewith. They neither reprove other men's lives nor glory in their own. These men, the more serviceable they behave themselves, the more they be honoured of all men. Yet they be divided into two sects. The one is of them that live single and chaste, abstaining not only from the company of women but also from eating of flesh, and some of them from all manner of beasts. Which, utterly rejecting the pleasures of this present life as hurtful, be all wholly set upon the desire of the life to come by watching and sweating, hoping shortly to obtain it, being in the mean season merry and lusty.

The other sect is no less desirous of labour; but they embrace matrimony, not despising the solace thereof, thinking that they cannot be discharged of their bounden duties towards nature without labour and toil nor towards their native country without procreation of children. They abstain from no pleasure that doth nothing hinder them from labour. They love the flesh of four-footed beasts because they believe that by that meat they be made hardier and stronger to work. The Utopians count this sect the wiser, but the other the holier. Which in that they prefer single life before matrimony and that sharp life before an easier life, if herein they grounded upon reason they would mock them. But now forasmuch as they say they be led to it by religion, they honour and worship them. And these be they whom in their language by a peculiar name they call Buthrescas, the which word by interpretation signifieth to us men of religion or religious men.

They have priests of exceeding holiness and therefore very few, for there be but thirteen in every city according to the number of their churches, saving when they go forth to battle. For then seven of them go forth with the army, in whose steads so many new be made at home. But the other at their return home again re-enter every one into his own place. They that be above the number, until such time as they succeed into the places of the other at their dying, be in the mean season continually in company with the bishop, for he is the chief head of them all. They be chosen of the people, as the other magistrates be, by secret voices for the avoiding of strife. After their election they be consecrate of their own company. They be overseers of all divine matters, orderers of religions, and, as it were, judges and masters of manners. And it is a great dishonesty and shame to be rebuked or spoken to by any of them for dissolute and incontinent living. But as it is their office to give good exhortations and counsel, so is it the duty of the prince and the other magistrates to correct and punish offenders, saving that the priests whom they find exceeding vicious livers, them they excommunicate from having any interest in divine matters. And there is almost no punishment among them more feared; for they run in very great infamy and be inwardly tormented with a secret fear of religion, and shall not long scape free with their bodies. For unless they by quick repentance approve the amendment of their lives to the priests, they be taken and punished of the council as wicked and irreligious.

Both childhood and youth is instructed and taught of them. Nor they be not more diligent to instruct them in learning than in virtue and good manners; for they use with very great endeavour and diligence to put into the heads of their children, whiles they be yet tender and pliant, good opinions and profitable for the conservation of their weal-public. Which, when they be once rooted in children, do remain with them all their life after and be wondrous profitable for the defence and maintenance of the state of the commonwealth, which never decayeth but through vices rising of evil opinions.

The priests, unless they be women (for that kind is not excluded from priesthood, howbeit few be chosen, and none but widows and old women), the men priests, I say, take to their wives the chiefest women in all their country; for to no office among the Utopians is more honour and pre-eminence given. Insomuch that if they commit any offence they be under no common judgment, but be left only to God and themselves. For they think it not lawful to touch him with man's hand, be he never so vicious, which after so singular a sort was dedicate and consecrate to God as a holy offering. This manner may they easily observe because they have so few priests, and do choose them with such circumspection. For it scarcely ever chanceth that the most virtuous among virtuous, which in respect only of his virtue is advanced to so high a dignity, can fall to vice and wickedness. And if it should chance indeed (as man's nature is mutable and frail), yet by reason they be so few and promoted to no might nor power, but only to honour, it were not to be feared that any great damage by them should happen and ensue to the commonwealth. They have so rare and few priests, lest if the honour were communicated to many, the dignity of the order, which among them now is so highly esteemed, should run in contempt; specially because they think it hard to find many so good as to be meet for that dignity, to the execution and discharge whereof it is not sufficient to be endued with mean virtues.

Furthermore, these priests be not more esteemed of their own countrymen than they be of foreign and strange countries. Which thing may hereby plainly appear, and I think also that this is the cause of it. For whiles the armies be fighting together in open field they a little beside, not far off, kneel upon their knees in their hallowed vestments, holding up their hands to heaven, praying first of all for peace, next for victory of their own part, but to neither part a bloody victory. If their host get the upper hand, they run into the main battle and restrain their own men from slaying and cruelly pursuing their vanquished enemies. Which enemies, if they do but see them and speak to them, it is enough for the safeguard of their lives. And the touching of their clothes defendeth and saveth all their goods from ravin and spoil. This thing hath avanced them to so great worship and true majesty among all nations, that many times they have as well preserved their own citizens from the cruel force of their enemies as they have their enemies from the furious rage of their own men. For it is well known that when their own army hath reculed, and in despair turned back and run away, their enemies fiercely pursuing with slaughter and spoil, then the priests coming between have stayed the murder and parted both the hosts, so that peace hath been made and concluded between both parts upon equal and indifferent conditions. For there was never any nation so fierce, so cruel, and rude but they had them in such reverence, that they counted their bodies hallowed and sanctified, and therefore not to be violently and unreverently touched.

They keep holy the first and the last day of every month and year, dividing the year into months which they measure by the course of the moon, as they do the year by the course of the sun. The first days they call in their language Cynemernes, and the last Trapemernes, the which words may be interpreted primifest and finifest, or else, in our speech, first feast and last feast. Their churches be very gorgeous, and not only of fine and curious workmanship, but also (which in the fewness of them was necessary) very wide and large, and able to receive a great company of people. But they be all somewhat dark. Howbeit, that was not done through ignorance in building, but, as they say, by the counsel of the priests, because they thought that overmuch light doth disperse men's cogitations, whereas in dim and doubtful light they be gathered together, and more earnestly fixed upon religion and devotion. Which because it is not there of one sort among all men, and yet all the kinds and fashions of it (though they be sundry and manifold) agree together in the honour of the divine nature, as going divers ways to one end, therefore nothing is seen nor heard in the churches, but that seemeth to agree indifferently with them all.

If there be a distinct kind of sacrifice peculiar to any several sect, that they execute at home in their own houses. The common sacrifices be so ordered that they be no derogation nor prejudice to any of the private sacrifices and religions. Therefore no image of any god is seen in the church, to the intent it may be free for every man to conceive God by their religion after what likeness and similitude they will. They call upon no peculiar name of God but only Mithra, in the which word they all agree together in one nature of the divine majesty whatsoever it be. No prayers be used but such as every man may boldly pronounce without the offending of any sect. They come, therefore, to the church the last day of every month and year, in the evening yet fasting, there to give thanks to God for that they have prosperously passed over the year or month whereof that holy day is the last day. The next day they come to the church early in the morning to pray to God that they may have good fortune and success all the new year or month which they do begin of that same holy day.

But in the holy days that be the last days of the months and years, before they come to the church the wives fall down prostrate before their husbands' feet at home, and the children before the feet of their parents, confessing and acknowledging themselves offenders either by some actual deed or by omission of their duty, and desire pardon for their offence. Thus if any cloud of privy displeasure was risen at home, by this satisfaction it is overblown, that they may be present at the sacrifices with pure and charitable minds. For they be afeard to come there with troubled consciences. Therefore if they know themselves to bear any hatred or grudge towards any man, they presume not to come to the sacrifices before they have reconciled themselves and purged their consciences, for fear of great vengeance and punishment for their offence. When they come thither the men go into the right side of the church and the women into the left side. There they place themselves in such order, that all they which be of the male kind in every household sit before the goodman of the house, and they of the female kind before the goodwife. Thus it is foreseen that all their gestures and behaviours be marked and observed abroad of them by whose authority and discipline they be governed at home. This also they diligently see unto, that the younger evermore be coupled with his elder, lest, children being joined together, they should pass over that time in childish wantonness, wherein they ought principally to conceive a religious and devout fear towards God, which is the chief and almost the only incitation to virtue.

They kill no living beast in sacrifice, nor they think not that the merciful clemency of God hath delight in blood and slaughter, which hath given life to beasts to the intent they should live. They burn frankincense and other sweet savours, and light also a great number of wax candles and tapers, not supposing this gear to be anything available to the divine nature, as neither the prayers of men; but this unhurtful and harmless kind of worship pleaseth them. And by these sweet savours and lights and other such ceremonies men feel themselves secretly lifted up and encouraged to devotion with more willing and fervent hearts. The people weareth in the church white apparel.

The priest is clothed in changeable colours, which in workmanship be excellent, but in stuff not very precious. For their vestments be neither embroidered with gold nor set with precious stones, but they be wrought so finely and cunningly with divers feathers of fowls, that the estimation of no costly stuff is able to countervail the price of the work. Furthermore, in these birds' feathers and in the due order of them which is observed in their setting, they say, is contained certain divine mysteries, the interpretation whereof known, which is diligently taught by the priests, they be put in remembrance of the bountiful benefits of God toward them, and of the love and honour which of their behalf is due to God, and also of their duties one toward another. When the priest first cometh out of the vestry thus apparelled, they fall down incontinent every one reverently to the ground with so still silence on every part, that the very fashion of the thing striketh into them a certain fear of God, as though He were there personally present. When they have lain a little space on the ground, the priest giveth them a sign for to rise. Then they sing praises unto God, which they intermix with instruments of music, for the most part of other fashions than these that we use in this part of the world. And like as some of ours be much sweeter than theirs, so some of theirs do far pass ours. But in one thing doubtless they go exceeding far beyond us. For all their music, both that they play upon instruments and that they sing with man's voice, doth so resemble and express natural affections, the sound and tune is so applied and made agreeable to the thing, that whether it be a prayer or else a ditty of gladness, of patience, of trouble, of mourning, or of anger, the fashion of the melody doth so represent the meaning of the thing, that it doth wonderfully move, stir, pierce, and inflame the hearers' minds. At the last the people and the priest together rehearse solemn prayers in words expressly pronounced, so made that every man may privately apply to himself that which is commonly spoken of all. In these prayers every man recognizeth and knowledgeth God to be his maker, his governor, and the principal cause of all other goodness, thanking Him for so many benefits received at His hand. But namely that through the favour of God he hath chanced into that public weal which is most happy and wealthy, and hath chosen that religion which he hopeth to be most true. In the which thing if he do anything err, or if there be any other better than either of them is, being more acceptable to God, he desireth Him that He will of His goodness let him have knowledge thereof, as one that is ready to follow what way soever He will lead him. But if this form and fashion of a commonwealth be best, and his own religion most true and perfect, then he desireth God to give him a constant steadfastness in the same, and to bring all other people to the same order of living and to the same opinion of God, unless there be anything that in this diversity of religions doth delight His unsearchable pleasure. To be short, he prayeth Him that after his death he may come to Him; but how soon or late, that he dare not assign or determine. Howbeit, if it might stand with His Majesty's pleasure, he would be much gladder to die a painful death and so to go to God, than by long living in worldly prosperity to be away from Him. When this prayer is said they fall down to the ground again, and a little after they rise up and go to dinner. And the residue of the day they pass over in plays and exercise of chivalry.

Now I have declared and described unto you as truly as I could the form and order of that commonwealth, which verily in my judgment is not only the best, but also that which alone of good right may claim and take upon it the name of a commonwealth or public weal. For in other places they speak still of the commonwealth, but every man procureth his own private gain. Here, where nothing is private, the common affairs be earnestly looked upon. And truly on both parts they have good cause so to do as they do; for in other countries who knoweth not that he shall starve for hunger, unless he make some several provision for himself, though the commonwealth flourish never so much in riches? And therefore he is compelled even of very necessity to have regard to himself rather than to the people, that is to say, to other. Contrariwise, there where all things be common to every man, it is not to be doubted that any man shall lack any thing necessary for his private uses, so that the common store, houses and barns, be sufficiently stored. For there nothing is distributed after a niggish sort, neither there is any poor man or beggar; and though no man have anything, yet every man is rich. For what can be more rich than to live joyfully and merrily, without all grief and pensiveness, not caring for his own living, nor vexed or troubled with his wife's importunate complaints, nor dreading poverty to his son, nor sorrowing for his daughter's dowry? Yea, they take no care at all for the living and wealth of themselves and all theirs, of their wives, their children, their nephews, their children's children, and all the succession that ever shall follow in their posterity. And yet, besides this, there is no less provision for them that were once labourers and be now weak and impotent, than for them that do now labour and take pain.

Here now would I see if any man dare be so bold as to compare with this equity the justice of other nations, among whom I forsake God if I can find any sign or token of equity and justice. For what justice is this, that a rich goldsmith or an usurer or, to be short, any of them which either do nothing at all, or else that which they do is such that it is not very necessary to the commonwealth, should have a pleasant and a wealthy living, either by idleness or by unnecessary business, when in the meantime poor labourers, carters, ironsmiths, carpenters, and plowmen (by so great and continual toil, as drawing and bearing beasts be scant able to sustain, and again so necessary toil, that without it no commonwealth were able to continue and endure one year), should yet get so hard and poor a living and live so wretched and miserable a life, that the state and condition of the labouring beasts may seem much better and wealthier? For they be not put to so continual labour, nor their living is not much worse, yea, to them much pleasanter, taking no thought in the mean season for the time to come. But these silly poor wretches be presently tormented with barren and unfruitful labour, and the remembrance of their poor, indigent, and beggarly old age killeth them up. For their daily wages is so little that it will not suffice for the same day, much less it yieldeth any overplus that may daily be laid up for the relief of old age.

Is not this an unjust and an unkind public weal, which giveth great fees and rewards to gentlemen, as they call them, and to goldsmiths and to such other, which be either idle persons, or else only flatterers and devisers of vain pleasures, and of the contrary part maketh no gentle provision for poor plowmen, colliers, labourers, carters, ironsmiths, and carpenters, without whom no commonwealth can continue? But after it hath abused the labours of their lusty and flowering age, at the last, when they be oppressed with old age and sickness, being needy, poor, and indigent of all things, then, forgetting their so many painful watchings, not remembering their so many and so great benefits, recompenseth and acquiteth them most unkindly with miserable death. And yet besides this the rich men, not only by private fraud but also by common laws, do every day pluck and snatch away from the poor some part of their daily living. So whereas it seemed before unjust to recompense with unkindness their pains that have been beneficial to the public weal, now they have to this their wrong and unjust dealing (which is yet a much worse point) given the name of justice, yea, and that by force of a law.

Therefore, when I consider and weigh in my mind all these commonwealths which nowadays anywhere do flourish, so God help me, I can perceive nothing but a certain conspiracy of rich men procuring their own commodities under the name and title of the common-wealth. They invent and devise all means and crafts, first how to keep safely, without fear of losing, that they have unjustly gathered together, and next how to hire and abuse the work and labour of the poor for as little money as may be. These devices, when the rich men have decreed to be kept and observed under colour of the commonalty, that is to say, also of the poor people, then they be made laws. But these most wicked and vicious men, when they have by their unsatiable covetousness divided among themselves all those things which would have sufficed all men, yet how far be they from the wealth and felicity of the Utopian commonwealth! Out of the which, in that all the desire of money with the use thereof is utterly secluded and banished, how great a heap of cares is cut away! How great an occasion of wickedness and mischief is plucked up by the roots! For who knoweth not that fraud, theft, ravin, brawling, quarrelling, brab-bling, strife, chiding, contention, murder, treason, poison-ing, which by daily punishments are rather revenged than refrained, do die when money dieth? And also that fear, grief, care, labours, and watchings do perish even the very same moment that money perisheth? Yea, poverty itself, which only seemed to lack money if money were gone, it also would decrease and vanish away.

And that you may perceive this more plainly, consider

with yourselves some barren and unfruitful year wherein many thousands of people have starved for hunger. I dare be bold to say that in the end of that penury so much corn or grain might have been found in the rich men's barns, if they had been searched, as, being divided among them whom famine and pestilence then consumed, no man at all should have felt that plague and penury. So easily might men get their living, if that same worthy princess Lady Money did not alone stop up the way between us and our living, which, a God's name, was very excellently devised and invented, that by her the way thereto should be opened. I am sure the rich men perceive this, nor they be not ignorant how much better it were to lack no necessary thing than to abound with overmuch superfluity, to be rid out of innumerable cares and troubles, than to be besieged and encumbered with great riches.

And I doubt not that either the respect of every man's private commodity, or else the authority of our Saviour Christ (which for His great wisdom could not but know what were best, and for His inestimable goodness could not but counsel to that which He knew to be best) would have brought all the world long ago into the laws of this weal-public, if it were not that one only beast, the princess and mother of all mischief, Pride, doth withstand and let it. She measureth not wealth and prosperity by her own commodities, but by the misery and incommodities of other. She would not by her goodwill be made a goddess if there were no wretches left over whom she might, like a scornful lady, rule and triumph, over whose miseries her felicities might shine, whose poverty she might vex, torment, and increase by gorgeously setting forth her riches. This hellhound creepeth into men's hearts and plucketh them back from entering the right path of life, and is so deeply rooted in men's breasts, that she cannot be plucked out.

This form and fashion of a weal-public, which I would gladly wish unto all nations, I am glad yet that it hath

chanced to the Utopians, which have followed those institutions of life whereby they have laid such foundations
of their commonwealth as shall continue and last not only
wealthily, but also, as far as man's wit may judge and
conjecture, shall endure for ever. For, seeing the chief
causes of ambition and sedition with other vices be
plucked up by the roots and abandoned at home, there
can be no jeopardy of domestical dissension, which alone
hath cast under foot and brought to naught the well forti-
fied and strongly defenced wealth and riches of many
cities. But forasmuch as perfect concord remaineth, and
wholesome laws be executed at home, the envy of all
foreign princes be not able to shake or move the empire,
though they have many times long ago gone about to do
it, being evermore driven back.

Thus when Raphael had made an end of his tale,
though many things came to my mind which in the manners and laws of that people seemed to be instituted and
founded of no good reason, not only in the fashion of
their chivalry and in their sacrifices and religions and in
other of their laws, but also, yea, and chiefly, in that which
is the principal foundation of all their ordinances, that is
to say, in the community of their life and living without
any occupying of money (by the which thing only all
nobility, magnificence, worship, honour, and majesty,
the true ornaments and honours, as the common opinion
is, of a commonwealth, utterly be overthrown and
destroyed), yet because I knew that he was weary of
talking, and was not sure whether he could abide that
anything should be said against his mind (specially
remembering that he had reprehended this fault in other,
which be afeard lest they should seem not to be wise
enough, unless they could find some fault in other men's
inventions), therefore I, praising both their institutions
and his communication, took him by the hand and led
him in to supper, saying that we would choose another
time to weigh and examine the same matters and to talk
with him more at large therein. Which would God it might

once come to pass. In the mean time, as I cannot agree and consent to all things that he said, being else without doubt a man singularly well learned and also in all worldly matters exactly and profoundly experienced, so must I needs confess and grant that many things be in the Utopian weal-public which in our cities I may rather wish for than hope for.

THUS ENDETH THE AFTERNOON'S TALK OF
RAPHAEL HYTHLODAY CONCERNING
THE LAWS AND INSTITUTIONS
OF THE ISLAND OF
UTOPIA.

HIEROME BUSLIDE

THOMAS MORE, the singular ornament of this our age, as you yourself (right honourable Buslide) can witness, to whom he is perfectly well known, sent unto me this other day the *Island of Utopia*, to very few as yet known, but most worthy. Which, as far excelling Plato's *Commonwealth*, all people should be willing to know: specially of a man most eloquent, so finely set forth, so cunningly painted out, and so evidently subject to the eye, that as oft as I read it, methinketh that I see somewhat more than when I heard Raphael Hythloday himself (for I was present at that talk as well as Master More) uttering and pronouncing his own words. Yea, though the same man according to his pure eloquence did so open and declare the matter, that he might plainly enough appear to report not things which he had learned of others only by hearsay, but which he had with his own eyes presently seen and thoroughly viewed, and wherein he had no small time been conversant and abiding: a man, truly, in mine opinion, as touching the knowledge of regions, peoples, and worldly experience, much passing, yea, even the very famous and renowned traveller Ulysses; and indeed such a one, as for the space of these 800 years past I think nature into the world brought not forth his like, in comparison of whom Vespucci may be thought to have seen nothing. Moreover, whereas we be wont more effectually and pithily to declare and express things that we have seen than which we have but only heard, there was besides that in this man a certain peculiar grace and singular dexterity to describe and set forth a matter withal.

Yet the selfsame things as oft as I behold and consider them drawn and painted out with Master More's pencil, I am therewith so moved, so delighted, so inflamed, and so rapt, that sometime methink I am presently conversant, even in the island of Utopia. And I promise you, I can scant believe that Raphael himself, by all that five years' space that he was in Utopia abiding, saw there so much as here in Master More's description is to be seen and perceived. Which description with so many wonders and miraculous things is replenished, that I stand in great doubt whereat first and chiefly to muse or marvel: whether at the excellency of his perfect and sure memory, which could wellnigh word by word rehearse so many things once only heard, or else at his singular prudence, who so well and wittily marked and bare away all the original causes and fountains (to the vulgar people commonly most unknown) whereof both issueth and springeth the mortal confusion and utter decay of a commonwealth and also the avancement and wealthy state of the same may rise and grow, or else at the efficacy and pith of his words which in so fine a Latin style, with such force of eloquence, hath couched together and comprised so many and divers matters, specially being a man continually encumbered with so many busy and troublesome cares, both public and private, as he is. Howbeit, all these things cause you little to marvel (right honourable Buslide) for that you are familiarly and thoroughly acquainted with the notable, yea, almost divine wit of the man.

But now to proceed to other matters, I surely know nothing needful or requisite to be adjoined unto his writings, only a metre of four verses written in the Utopian tongue, which after Master More's departure Hythloday by chance shewed me, that have I caused to be added thereto, with the alphabet of the same nation, and have also garnished the margin of the book with certain notes. For, as touching the situation of the island, that is to say, in what part of the world Utopia standeth, the ignorance and lack whereof not a little troubleth and grieveth

Master More, indeed Raphael left not that unspoken of. Howbeit, with very few words he lightly touched it, incidentally by the way passing it over, as meaning of likelihood to keep and reserve that to another place. And the same, I wot not how, by a certain evil and unlucky chance escaped us both. For when Raphael was speaking thereof, one of Master More's servants came to him and whispered in his ear. Wherefore, I being then of purpose more earnestly addict to hear, one of the company, by reason of cold taken, I think, a-shipboard, coughed out so loud, that he took from my hearing certain of his words. But I will never stint nor rest until I have got the full and exact knowledge hereof, insomuch that I will be able perfectly to instruct you, not only in the longitude or true meridian of the island, but also in the just latitude thereof, that is to say, in the sublevation or height of the pole in that region, if our friend Hythloday be in safety and alive. For we hear very uncertain news of him. Some report that he died in his journey homeward. Some again affirm that he returned into his country; but partly for that he could not away with the fashions of his country folk, and partly for that his mind and affection was altogether set and fixed upon Utopia, they say that he hath taken his voyage thitherward again. Now as touching this, that the name of this island is nowhere found among the old and ancient cosmographers, this doubt Hythloday himself very well dissolved. For why, it is possible enough, quoth he, that the name which it had in old time was afterward changed, or else that they never had knowledge of this island, forasmuch as now in our time divers lands be found which to the old geographers were unknown. Howbeit, what needeth it in this behalf to fortify the matter with arguments, seeing Master More is author hereof sufficient? But whereas he doubteth of the edition or imprinting of the book, indeed herein I both commend and also knowledge the man's modesty. Howbeit, unto me it seemeth a work most unworthy to be long suppressed and most worthy to go abroad into the hands of men; yea, and under the title of your name to be published to the world, either because the singular endowments and qualities of Master More be to no man better known than to you, or else because no man is more fit and meet than you with good counsels to further and advance the commonwealth, wherein you have many years already continued and travailed with great glory and commendation, both of wisdom and knowledge, and also of integrity and uprightness. Thus, O liberal supporter of good learning, and flower of this our time, I bid you most heartily well to fare. At Antwerp 1516, the first day of November.

A METRE OF FOUR VERSES IN THE UTOPIAN TONGUE,

Briefly touching as well the strange beginning, as also the happy and wealthy continuance of the same commonwealth

Utopos ha Boccas peu la chama polta chamaan.
Bargol he maglomi baccan soma gymnosophaon.
Agrama gymnosophon labarem bacha bodamilomin.
Volvala barchin heman la lavolvala dramme pagloni.

Which verses the translator, according to his simple knowledge and mean understanding in the Utopian tongue, hath thus rudely englished.

My king and conqueror Utopos by name,
A prince of much renown and immortal fame,
Hath made me an isle that erst no island was,
Full fraught with worldly wealth, with pleasure and solace.
I one of all other without philosophy
Have shaped for man a philosophical city.
As mine I am nothing dangerous to impart,
So better to receive I am ready with all my heart.

A short metre of Utopia, written by Anemolius poet laureate and nephew to Hythloday by his sister

Me Utopie cleped Antiquity,
Void of haunt and herborough,
Now am I like to Plato's city,
Whose fame flieth the world thorough;
Yea, like, or rather more likely
Plato's plat to excel and pass.
For what Plato's pen hath platted briefly
In naked words, as in a glass,
The same have I performed fully,
With laws, with men, and treasure fitly.
Wherefore not Utopie, but rather rightly
My name is Eutopie: a place of felicity.

Gerard Noviomage of Utopia

Doth pleasure please? Then place thee here, and well thee
    rest;
Most pleasant pleasures thou shalt find here.
Doth profit ease? Then here arrive, this isle is best.
For passing profits do here appear.
Doth both thee tempt, and wouldst thou grip both gain and
    pleasure?
This isle is fraught with both bounteously.
To still thy greedy intent, reap here incomparable treasure
Both mind and tongue to garnish richly.
The hid wells and fountains both of vice and virtue
Thou hast them here subject unto thine eye.
Be thankful now, and thanks where thanks be due:
Give to Thomas More London's immortal glory.

Cornelius Graphey to the Reader

Wilt thou know what wonders strange be in the land that
    late was found?
Wilt thou learn thy life to lead by divers ways that godly be?
Wilt thou of virtue and of vice understand the very ground?
Wilt thou see this wretched world, how full it is of vanity?
Then read and mark and bear in mind for thy behoof, as
    thou may best,
All things that in this present work, that worthy clerk Sir
    Thomas More,
With wit divine full learnedly unto the world hath plain
    exprest,
In whom London well glory may, for wisdom and for godly
    lore.

THE PRINTER TO THE READER

THE Utopian alphabet, good reader, which in the above written epistle is promised, hereunto I have not now adjoined, because I have not as yet the true characters or forms of the Utopian letters. And no marvel, seeing it is a tongue to us much stranger than the Indian, the Persian, the Syrian, the Arabic, the Egyptian, the Macedonian, the Sclavonian, the Cyprian, the Scythian, etc. Which tongues, though they be nothing so strange among us as the Utopian is, yet their characters we have not. But I trust, God willing, at the next impression hereof, to perform that which now I cannot: that is to say, to exhibit perfectly unto thee the Utopian alphabet. In the meantime accept my goodwill. And so farewell.

GLOSSARY

ACHORIANS, placeless folk

ADVENTURE, chance; AT ADVENTURE, at random, recklessly

AFFECTION, partiality

AFFIANCE, confidence

ALAOPOLITANS, community of blind folk

ALLIANT, akin

AMAUROTE, faint-seen

ANEMOLIANS, windy folk

ANYDER, waterless

APPAIRED, impaired

ASTONIED, deprived of the power to act, dazed

AUNTERS, IN, if perchance

AVAUNT, to boast

AVOUTRERS, AVOUTRY, adulterers, adultery

BEAR THE SWING, to have full control

BECK, gesture notifying a command

BRABBLING, contention

BUTHRESCAS, very religious folk

CAREFUL, full of cares

CARK, to assume a burden

CAUTEL, quibble

CAVILLATION, useless or mocking objection

CERTES, assuredly

CHAFFARE, barter, trade

COMMODITY, convenience

CONCEDES, fancy dishes

CONVERSANT, habitually residing

CONVEYANCE, expression

COVIN, deceit, collusion

CUNNING, knowledgeable

DIZZARDS, blockheads

DORS, drones

EFTSOONS, again, afterwards

EMBRAID, to upbraid

ESPIAL, a spy

EXISTIMATION, repute

FARDEL, bundle, load

FOINS, thrusts

FORBY, past

FRAY, to frighten

GALLIMAUFRY, jumble or medley

GEAR, means of living, goods

GENTLE, generous, courteous

GLEBELAND, portion of land going with clergyman's benefice

GRAMERCY, a thank-you

GYVES, shackles or fetters

HAPT, wrapped

HAUNT, a place of frequent resort or usual abode

HAUT, high, haughty

HERBOROUGH, harbour

HYTHLODAY, nonsense-talker

INCONTINENT, forthwith

INDIFFERENT, just, impartial

INFAMED, accused, disgraced

JAVEL, good-for-nothing

JET, to swagger

KNOWLEDGE, to acknowledge

LET, hindrance, impediment; to hinder, forbear, refrain
LEWD, untrained, unlettered; perverse
LOUTING, mocking

MACARIANS, happy folk
MATTOCK, pick-shaped agricultural tool
MISLIKE, to displease
MURRAIN, infectious disease in farm animals

NEPHELOGETES, cloud folk
NIGGISH, niggardly
NOYOUS, vexatious, troublesome

OCCUPY, to make use of (money), carry on (craft), deal (with)
OVERTHWART, perverse; across

PARDY, in truth, surely
PASS, to care (about), concern oneself (with); to surpass
PENNY-FATHERS, skinflints
PICK A THANK, to curry favour
PILL, to pillage
PLAT, plan
POLYERITES, very nonsensical folk
PRESENTLY, on the spot, at once
PRETENCE, design
PROOF, fulfilment, thriving

PUISSANCE, great power, might
PULLEN, fowl

QUAILED, enfeebled

RAMPIER, to strengthen by a rampart
RAVIN, rapine, plunder
RECULED, recoiled, retreated
ROOM, space; office, employment
RUSHBUCKLERS, swashbucklers

SAD, serious, sober
SEMBLABLE, like
SEVERAL, apart, separate
SKILL, to matter
SPILL, to ruin, destroy
STRAIT, narrow, strict
SUIT, pursuit
SWING, BEAR THE, see BEAR THE SWING

TABLE, picture; TABLES, backgammon
TAPROBANE, Ceylon
THRONG, crowded
TRANSLATING, transferring

UPLANDISH, rustic
UTOPIA, nowhere

WARE, aware, beware
WARRANTISE, surety, guarantee
WEAL, welfare
WIPED, defrauded
WITTILY, wisely, cleverly
WRITHEN, twisted

ZAPOLETES, great gadabouts

ABOUT THE INTRODUCER

JENNY MEZCIEMS is Senior Lecturer in English at the University of Warwick.

ABOUT THE TRANSLATOR

Very little is known of Ralph Robinson. He was born in 1521, one of a large and poor family, and was a fellow pupil of William Cecil, the future Lord Burghley (as he mentions in his dedicatory letter) at Grantham and Stamford Grammar Schools. He went to Oxford (he describes himself, on the title page to the second edition, as 'sometime fellow of Corpus Christi College') and afterwards came to London where he obtained the livery of the Goldsmiths' Company and was employed in a minor clerical capacity in Cecil's office. His translation of Utopia, the first in English, was published in 1551, and revised by him in 1556. The date of his death is uncertain.

This book is set in CASLON, designed and engraved by William
Caslon of WILLIAM CASLON & SON, Letter-Founders in
London, around 1740. In England at the beginning of
the eighteenth century, Dutch type was probably
more widely used than English. The rise
of William Caslon put a stop to the
importation of Dutch types
and so changed the his-
tory of English
typecutting.